MINOR ILLUSIONS

Minor Illusions

Daryl Li

QUERENCIA

Querencia Press – Chicago IL

QUERENCIA PRESS

ISBN 978 1 963943 61 0

www.querenciapress.com

First Published in 2025

Querencia Press, LLC
Chicago IL

Printed & Bound in the United States of America

I'M AFRAID OF AN EXTRA FACE
IN THE MIRROR AND SUDDEN
NIGHTS WITH VOICES, THE DEEP
CERTAINTY OF THINGS.

—SALVADOR ESPRIU, *PARCA*

YOU MAY NOT BELIEVE IN MAGIC BUT SOMETHING VERY STRANGE IS HAPPENING AT THIS VERY MOMENT. YOUR HEAD HAS DISSOLVED INTO THIN AIR AND I CAN SEE THE RHODODENDRONS THROUGH YOUR STOMACH. IT'S NOT THAT YOU ARE DEAD OR ANYTHING DRAMATIC LIKE THAT, IT IS SIMPLY THAT YOU ARE FADING AWAY AND I CAN'T EVEN REMEMBER YOUR NAME.

—LEONORA CARRINGTON, *THE HEARING TRUMPET*

Contents

MYTHOLOGIES

The Puppets

The thread is his way back. She was specific: Only down, never left, never right. He follows this to the letter, charting a path through this maze. What's the point of all this? he wonders. What sort of hero merely adheres to instructions? In fact, what is this heroic impulse? Why was his destiny to be a hero? Then he finds the magnificent beast, its eyes betraying the weight of an equally monstrous fate. Theseus extends a hand. "Hello, my friend," he says. "Come with me. If we follow this thread out of here, we can both be free."

Lives of the Immortals

Today it will be different. Today something will come between us. No, not me and that pitiful creature ahead of me. Me and the Fates—or the philosophies. Something will stop this accursed race without rhyme or reason. Today, this will finally end. Some conclusion drawn. Some work finished.

Then again, today goes on forever. That's the whole point.

Yes, yes, laugh all you want at the absurdity of this scene. Brave Achilles and a bloody tortoise, one chasing the other down in a—

Where are we in the first place? What have we even been running on? Dirt, sand, a wilted tree I see out of the corner of my eye. Is this what you see too? Is this what you imagine? This endless track, leading perhaps nowhere, perhaps everywhere, as a realistic landscape scrolls by. Realistic, yes, but also plain, nondescript, something completely naturalistic. A vision of relativity, for in infinity, the landscape travels past us as much as we pass it by.

This is what a paradox looks like. Zeno's Paradox, to be exact. Plain and uninteresting and patently absurd. A complete waste of everyone's time. Stop looking. Forget me. I've had enough.

I've done it all: I've slain men, monsters, and monstrous men, tackled the greatest warriors, and battled gods. I've died (in multiple ways) and seen Hades—both the person and the place. I've even had a cult. I mean, I claim no ownership over it, but they seemed to believe that it was what I wanted. I must profess that I know very little of their practices. For all I know, they worshipped heels. They must have elevated me to some kind of lofty stature based on vague interpretive concepts they had adopted, like all other cults. Perhaps they believed that there was something heroic in me. Or perhaps they were into the violence. I couldn't do anything about it. I was at the mercy of these hobbyists and the strength of their collective conviction.

But what I mean is, I've had an eventful life, and certainly a relatively pleasant afterlife too. How many other Greek heroes can claim to have been played by Brad Pitt? What was that line again? Immortality? Take it? It's yours? Yes, that's what he said. That's what I was supposed to have said, what I must have said, what I couldn't not have said. Now that everyone thinks I said it, I must have said it. That fight with

Hector has become a filmic classic. It's not at all true to how the fight unfolded, of course. I'm sure I didn't humiliate him as much. Or perhaps I did. Memory is hard to trust. Brad's spear technique is also wrong, and he had very little of a warrior in him. But I understand that. I understand fight choreography and dramatization. I understand the need to be flashy. I understand that reality is often much less thrilling. I've spent several lifetimes just becoming stories after all. And to be honest, I don't mind these stories. Better these than that sod who has to keep rolling that boulder up the hill. Better these than that eagle that has to eat the same damned liver every damned night. I've had a full life, yes—or what would be a full life if it hadn't simply continued into forever. Look at me. Every moment is a dilution, every use of my name a citation, every image a gradual hollowing out of my being.

From birth, I was destined for immortality. My father was a king, a friend to Heracles, and a brute in love. My mother was of the sea, and he claimed her affections only with the advice of Proteus and a stubborn grip that overcame her best efforts at escape. So much for consent. Thus, was written the great romance of Peleus and Thetis. Families are always trouble. Just look at Zeus and his complicated family tree.

When I was an infant, my mother decided that I should have the gift of invulnerability, just one step removed from immortality. So down I went, headfirst, into the river Styx.

Mother knows best, as they say. But did she really? I mean, I sometimes wished that she had asked for my consent, but I guess she learnt a thing or two from my father. The truth is, how could a goddess, who has only ever known immortality, ever hope to understand the depravity of such a thing? You don't suddenly develop empathy for mortals.

Mother did not realize that I would live forever. And I *have* lived forever, in a manner of speaking. The philosophers will tell you that no one can live forever because you'll never reach the end of it to say that you truly have done so. That is the problem of infinity. You can't put a cap on it. It just goes on forever. But you know what I mean. It's the twenty-first century and I'm still here chasing after a godforsaken tortoise.

Time is a cruel joke.

How long have I been running? No, I don't want to know that. Not really. I was born some three or four thousand years ago but this invention of Zeno happened almost a whole millennium after my birth, which only goes to show who's in charge of your life. Take the example of Pythagoras, who likely had very little to do with the famed theorem but somehow managed to put his name on it and in textbooks worldwide. Like me, he had his fair share of cults too, revered as some sort of grand teacher or eccentric genius, depending on who you ask. Today, he commands less attention than the theorem that bears his name. In contrast, I've survived with the general arcs of my biography intact. They have weathered natural disasters, great wars, and even the advent of the information age. Take my word for it, if you ever wanted to live forever and you ever had a choice, always choose drama over knowledge, myth over science. Stories enable one to survive much better than mathematical formulae.

Sometimes, however, I wonder if we're really all that different. I mean, I'm stuck in this meaningless paradox. Initially, I was flattered. I've been the hero of many stories, even if sometimes what counts as heroic is questionable at best. But a direct philosophical question? That was new to me. I enjoyed it. I liked being associated with a different kind of education— logical, philosophical, perhaps mathematical. At least, it seemed like a nice bargain to me at first. But I didn't realize then that I would be locked forever in the human imagination, becoming party to that accursed Zeno's stupid mind games. Had we lived in the same era I would have ensured that this would never come to pass, poised my spear right at his heart and driven the tip straight through to the other side. You who have given me eternal life. All of you.

Do you understand? I don't want to live forever. If I could choose to die, I would die now. I've had a good run—I mean, a good life. This is not a good run. I used to love running. You barely even feel it when your body's machinery is so well-tuned. Most gods are projections of human aspects, but so are heroes and villains, just archetypes. Perhaps this is true of my physique, an expression of elysian inspiration. Flawless, ideal, something beyond human, beyond time.

As you can imagine, I no longer feel the same way about running. I just wish it would end now. It used to be a celebration of the divine engineering underneath this marvellous form, but by the heavens, how I detest it today. There is very little left for me in this body I inhabit. I am no longer what I am, only what I represent: a body that is not a body, but a symbol of perfection. Perfection, like divinity, lies outside the concept of time. Yet, here I am, hardly a god, yet trapped in a kind of undecaying forever, a kind of monotonous undeath.

Immortality is a curse and I don't even suffer from the worst of it. I don't live with eternal hunger like Erysichthon or the gruesome, cursed biology of Lamia. I am not punished. My life has comparatively minor tragedies, and my body is fine. No, it is more than fine. Gaze upon this Apollonian countenance. Behold this expertly toned frame, this well-oiled machine, bolting forth, tearing through the air, and know that it is little more than a disgusting ideal.

I don't get why some people want to live forever. I suppose it betrays a great fear of the unknown, or perhaps an aspirational side to humankind to hang onto everything they have, or an understanding of the transience of life. Here, however, on this endless track, where there is little meaning or purpose, forever is cosmically frightening. I exist between the stories and the impressions, the sketches and the meanings, in the moments between moments, in the split seconds.

I'm sorry. You're not used to such a defeatist Achilles, and I understand. You've heard the stories about me. But think about it: The thing I'm most famous for these days is a weakness in the heel. And can you blame me; with all the running I've been made to do? Maybe it is a form of repetitive strain injury. These days you have running shoes, some apparently marketed by the goddess Nike. If only she would deign to bless me with some of those now. You're not used to a talkative, unheroic, deflated Achilles who thinks too much. You expected someone more muscular, more vigorous, more warrior-like, not someone lost in stagnant thought about infinity and immortality. But in the lives of the immortals, one has nothing if not an excess of time. I've had plenty of time to sort out my ideas, think about my plight. There's no one to save and no one left to fight. Hundreds and hundreds of years and there's nothing left. The only things we accumulate are scars and trauma and forgetfulness. A hollow shape, unable to even summon a ghost of the person I am supposed to be.

I have been forced to abandon all substance, all bodily pretences, trapped in this endless race, this unsolvable question, this farce. There's really nothing to it, is there? Just Achilles and a damned tortoise. Tortoises aren't even scary or impressive, except maybe for their age. Why aren't they extinct? They seem so utterly useless, so slow and so harmless, only capable of eating vegetables and little else, barely more than helmet fodder. Here you are, you wretched creature, taunting me with your lack of speed, your invincible impotence. Look at you, so smug in the safety of this infinite distance. So comfortable in your uselessness. I will defeat you. All of you. I'll kill every one of you. I'll . . . I'll . . .

I apologize. My emotions got the better of me. This is absolutely no fault of this tortoise, an exemplary example of a marvellous species that has survived for millions and millions of years. That's nothing compared to the vast expanse of infinity, but certainly it would know one or two things about immortal existence. Its kind has existed since an age prehistoric, a time long before stories. The tortoise is innocent. All it's doing is fulfilling its role in its ecological niche. It's just a part of a complicated system of many moving parts. What's worse is, it has no personality, no purpose in life, no dramatic arc. It doesn't even have a name. I'm not even sure it's real. It feels more like a symbol or a joke, placed here in this meaningless situation to mock me in a turn of comical irony, a tool in the selfish economy of human stories, circular and circulating.

Besides, if the tortoise beat the hare, what chance have I got? Immortal or not, humans don't run much faster than their machinery allows. Even Usain Bolt doesn't run faster than a hare, and his name is Bolt. The tortoise has survived both as species and story. It is resilient, evolutionarily stubborn, and also culturally popular.

Apart from that ridiculous race and this cursed paradox, there are many references to them where I come from. It is said, for instance, that it was Zeus who messed around with wildlife because he can't keep his hands and moral compass to himself, blessing the tortoise with the burden of forever having to carry its shell. Aesop had a real optimistic outlook. As though blissfully ignorant of the cruelty of gods and their humour, he believed that this meant the tortoise would always carry its home sweet home, like some counterpoint to Odysseus, who only felt at home when he was away from home. 'Twas also a tortoise that fell on Aeschylus, killing the poor man. What the bird was doing with such a heavy reptile in its talons eludes me, but had the dramatist survived longer, perhaps his trilogy about me would have survived. The tortoise was also the weapon of choice of Sciron, a nefarious bandit who was only defeated by Theseus when he sent him into the sea. Poetic justice, Theseus said. Never liked the guy. Like a prototype for yours truly. I suppose all stories have drafts, all creations have prototypes, all theses start from rough ideas. Whatever it is, look closely at its history and you can see that the tortoise's mythic history is all curse and murder. All right, I concede that it is occasionally a fertility symbol, but you get my point.

I don't hate you, wretched creature. We both are wretched creatures. You're my oldest friend. You're the only one who understands what it is to be trapped in this eternity. My feet grow heavier with each step. I'm so tired. I should go for a holiday. Somewhere where there's rain for once, and more wildlife than a tortoise. Anywhere except Paris. I'm lonely too. I miss Patroclus. Barely anyone remembers dear Patroclus, the paver of ways, the keeper of secrets. Why couldn't they at least have remembered us together? Was it a distaste for the connection we shared? Was he just less attractive as a heroic figure? He has not passed into the zeitgeist in the same way. In fact, it was that damned Bard of yours, that William, who turned our friendship into a bawdy tale. And now all I have is the company of a reptile.

Step into my non-Nike shoes for a moment. Understand my suffering. I am no longer who I am. I am unable to be who I am. Here and now, I am not Achilles of the Trojan War. I am not Achilles of the Grecian warriors. I am not infant, boy, enemy, or hero. I am story, I am myth, I am convenient metaphor for logical experiments. I am image and sign, a role in a movie. I am nothing but form and function. My station is now myth, archetype, and trope. I'm a hero only because of the stories. I'm a joke only because of the stories. It's all the stories. Once flesh and blood, now just words, now just fable, now just an immortal image projected on digital screens.

I don't want your Homeric odes. They're all just lies. Do you understand? I don't want to be an amusement or a piece in an unsolvable puzzle. This form is but a constructed form. This body, churning, twisting, suffering, is but the thinnest veneer, bound in endlessness, chasing without catching, advancing without advancing.

Perhaps today, I will finally be a hero, capable of wrestling with tyrant destiny. How does a man change his fate? The few who have dared have only found tragedy. The Theban king Oedipus. His daughter Antigone. Andromache. Hector and Patroclus. And myself. Victims of destiny. I just want to take a break. I just want to catch my breath. Atropos, why have you abandoned me? Can I stop running now? Can my life finally come to an end? Can you forget me now? Immortality, yes, take it. Please. It's yours.

Today it will be different. Today I will finally be free. Today, plastic Achilles will pierce that impenetrable cloak of stories. I have this feeling in my bones. I can see it in my mind's eye. I let the vision propel me forth, let desire take hold one more time, blind belief. I can see the deformations on its shell, smell its musty scent. I can see myself charging through the air, closing the distance.

Indeed, the distance seems to be shrinking. Impossible. After so long? What has changed? How are my feet finally catching up with the reptile? Who has authored this twist of fate? Is this another one of your cruel jokes? No matter, no matter. I've done it. I don't know how, but I've done it. This ends now. I've caught up with the wretched tortoise. I'll wring its neck, put it out of its misery, put me out of my misery. Finally this story can come to an end. I tremble as I entertain the thought. What awaits on the other side of the paradox?

It turns and looks right at me. I stare at its antediluvian face, the eyes that seem to carry more wisdom than my entire civilization. A creature as ancient as I am immortal. Its carapace catches a drop of the sun. Around us, things fall into silence. A tense moment arrives, persists. A chilling breeze. Some recognition of our common plight. Some mutual understanding. And in my mind, in our minds, we ask the same questions: Has this story ended? Who's telling this tale now?

The Same Old Story

One morning, Mother told her three sons to pack their things, leave the house, and make a living for themselves. Things had been difficult ever since Father left the family, and it hadn't been easy raising three children by herself. She was tired, and now that they had grown old enough to have a shot at independence, she felt that it was time to retire. She simply wanted to be alone. Perhaps a little too enthusiastically, the three children got ready. The sun was just rising as they stepped out of the door. The three children had more than a dash of trepidation in their hearts. They were hungry for success, for adventure, and for food, but it was a large forest, and there were many others who were hungry too—especially for pork chops.

Thus, the three pigs went their separate ways, leaving Mother behind in an old rocking chair. Several days after he had left the house, Pig One encountered a man who carried with him a heap of straw. Feeling as though the stars had aligned, the pig did not hesitate to ask the man for all of his straw. "I need to build a house," he said, "and that straw will do nicely."

The man threw his arms up in the air, depositing the straw on the ground, and ran off to enjoy his spring. A truly charitable person. Or perhaps it was just the shock of this encounter with a talking pig.

Unfortunately, Pig One demonstrated quite impressively all the stereotypes we associate with porcine kind: He was fat, lazy, and unintelligent. Hence, he built a terrible house. This had nothing to do with his choice of building material. He simply had neither the talent nor the industry. This spelt trouble when one day a wolf came to visit, because it was a big bad wolf.

The Big Bad Wolf, stomach growling, said, "Little pig, little pig, let me come in." Surely, he was being courteous, since Pig One, pot belly and all, could hardly be considered little.

Pig One thanked him for the compliment, before saying, "No, no, not by the hair on my chinny, chin, chin." (He had forgotten to shave that morning.)

So the Big Bad Wolf threatened, "Then I'll huff, and I'll puff, and I'll blow your house in."

As soon as he said that, the wolf took in a miraculously deep breath, causing his chest to swell like a toad's. Then he exhaled and the pig's house was swept away in a gust of foul stench.

Pig One stood in the open, naked, scared, and looking more delicious than he had ever looked in his entire life. He was well aware of his impending doom, and it terrified him that he would soon greet the great unknown. Just then, however, he was possessed by a sense of destiny. As he looked at the glistening canines of his visitor, he reasoned that it must all have been part of some divine plan. Why else were there three pigs? Surely there must have been a grand design leading to some terrific conclusion based on the rule of three. It was unfortunate that he had to go, but he accepted this with all the gusto of a willing sacrifice. Besides, what were pigs good for if they weren't meant to be eaten by wolves? He wanted to die smiling, but the bite really hurt.

Earlier, on a different and splendid morning, Pig Two met a man. He had to squint because the sun was behind the man. It may in fact have been the same man, but we will never know because the sun made it hard to see. On this occasion, he was carrying a large bundle of sticks. Like his brother, Pig Two decided to ask for help with his house. The man readily agreed to surrender his sticks. How charitable. Or perhaps it was just the uncanniness of déjà vu.

Pig Two built a much better house than his brother because he had a sound design. He also worked fast, such that by the time the Big Bad Wolf had visited and eaten his brother, Pig Two had long completed his sturdy stick mansion. Speaking of the Big Bad Wolf, it had been barely two hours since he had devoured the first pig when he chanced upon the second one.

Wolves being wolves, he was determined to swallow Pig Two as well.

Because he hadn't the wit to think of something new to say, the Big Bad Wolf bellowed, "Little pig, little pig, let me come in."

Pig Two was indeed little. He replied, "No, no, not by the hair on my chinny, chin, chin."

This surprised the wolf because it was precisely the same thing that the first pig had said. Déjà vu, as mentioned above, can be a most frightening thing. Seized by a sense of the uncanny, the wolf found himself unable to speak. He began to think that he was imagining things. Was he suffering from a bout of carnivore's guilt? In his paranoia, he feared that he was simply some character in a story. He remembered the recurring dream of his in which he chomped on the flock of a young, lying shepherd. Initially, he had passed it off as some wild fantasy, but he now understood that it was a message. All his life he had been an accessory, and he was sick of it. He didn't want to be just necessary. He wanted to live for himself. Thus, the Big Bad Wolf groaned (leaving Pig Two very confused). He decided that he would no longer be a tool to a dramatic story, an accessory to murder, and a slave to the food chain. Besides, he was a little full.

Rubbing his noticeable tummy, he said, "I've had my fill. I'm going home." And so, he turned back, dragging his feet as he walked away from Pig Two's impressive mansion of sticks. The pig was disappointed. Here he was on the cusp of his big moment, ready to step into his role as prey. It would eventually plunge him into clinically certifiable depression, and he would spend many of his remaining days attempting to get eaten.

Meanwhile, farther down the road, Pig Three had built his own house too. Some days ago, he had encountered an exceptionally strong man carrying so many bricks that one could build a cottage out of it. The man was wearing a large hat, and it was impossible to see his face under the shade. Without a word, he dumped the bricks at the feet of the pig and left. Pig Three supposed he had had enough. So this little piggy worked day and night to construct his little cottage. He was the most diligent of the lot, and if the Big Bad Wolf had decided to come by immediately after visiting both his brothers, he would be greeted by a most remarkable stone cottage. There was a kitchen with some pans and a large pot. There were two showers, a cozy bedroom, and a living room where one could play a game of billiards. He even built an exquisite fireplace and a nice chimney.

In the days that followed, Pig Three lived happily in his abode. He earned an honest keep and was well-liked and respected in his community. He spent most of his free time gardening and reading. Eventually, he got married to a good girl and they had three children. He never broke the law. He raised his children well. He helped his neighbors. Suffice to say, he became an upstanding and productive member of society. It was a good life, if a tad boring. Now and then, he would think of his mother. He would stare into space with a strange expression on his face, as if awaiting a denouement that would never arrive.

The Puppeteer

Tonight, on this hill, the young boy will die. But you already know that. He will be chased through your choice of vegetation: reed and thistle, temperate woods, or dense vegetation—though to be geographically accurate, perhaps it should be some kind of rainforest. Doesn't matter. It's all up to you.

The boy is being pursued by soldiers from the palace in the dead of night. By proposing an ingenious solution to the problem of unnaturally aggressive swordfish plaguing the fishermen involving banana tree trunks, he has gravely offended the ruling sultan. That the plan had worked has caused the insecure ruler to descend into a paranoid state, and now, the man fears that he will soon be displaced by a child.

As long as these details remain intact, everything else is in the telling. Improvisation. Jazz. Omakase. It's all up to you.

You may also choose to vary the way in which he is killed, although due to the necessary outcomes, you must ensure that an egregious amount of blood is spilled so that it may dye the hill, thus creating the red hill that is central to this tale, Bukit Merah. Poison, for instance, is generally unacceptable, although it is possible that it results in the boy spewing blood— a tad dramatic but perhaps not unreasonable given the tragic nature of this tale.

In this way, the boy will live forever, but he will also die and die again. There are tales recited so often that they have become rote, stories told so many times that they have become true. Indeed, each retelling further commits this story to a shared truth, one that will survive the grand decay of time, immortal.

He has been here before. Having experienced his death time and again, he understands that in the grandeur of myth and the structures of stories, there is no room for the life of a little boy whose name is lost to the sweeping tides of history. There is only erasure.

Or perhaps, one of these days, he will be able to escape the finality of fate. Perhaps he will be able to choose to live. Perhaps he will be more than a tale, stepping out of the boundaries so long inscribed for him. The thought thrills. He becomes nervous. Maybe this is the day. Or maybe not.

It's all up to you.

FICTIONS

A Secret Literature: The Literature of Ong Hwee Teng and the Possibilities of Disappearance

[Name withheld for submission][1]

"In order to understand, I destroyed myself."

Fernando Pessoa[2]

INTRODUCTION

The topics of erasure, nothingness, and disappearance have a long artistic and critical history in literature. From Sappho's fragments to Beckett's silences, Hegel to Derrida, our

---

[1] "No name, address or identifying marks other than the title and NRIC number should be indicated in the manuscript."

[2] Fernando Pessoa (as Bernardo Soares), *The Book of Disquiet*, edited by Maria José de Lancastre, translated by Margaret Jull Costa (London: Serpent's Tail, 1991), p. 147.

fascination with the void has survived both time and radical shifts in discourse, and arguably, has only intensified in the past century.

In this essay, I present an overview of the work of Singaporean writer Ong Hwee Teng against a background of such topics. Ong can be considered to be a member of the recent New Singaporean Literature phenomenon, which has been described by Joanne Wee as "a term of convenience banding together writers who are mostly relatively new to the Singaporean literature scene under a vague impression of similar ethos"[3]. New Singaporean Literature cannot be considered a literary movement, even if it bears a definite resemblance to one. Spontaneously formed and without a unified sense of purpose, the work of its writers is typically in English, even if notable exceptions exist. There is also a preference for challenging literature, favouring a high degree of complexity in plot and form. Additionally, the works show an inclination towards the fantastic. The writers also have a tendency to avoid interaction with the literary scene outside of New Singaporean Literature.

---

[3] Joanne Wee, "'There's No Art': Considering New Singaporean Literature as a Literary Movement" in Dennis Goh ed., *Critical Essays on New Singaporean Literature* (Singapore: National University of Singapore Press, 2010), p. 39.

The main aim of this paper is to serve as an introduction to Ong's work. As such an introduction has been lacking in the existing literature. I will proceed by using the themes of erasure and nothingness that are prominent in her work. Specifically, I trace the development of Ong's fascination with these themes in a chronological fashion based on her bibliography. At the same time, I hope to contribute to the slowly growing corpus of critical writing on New Singaporean Literature.

EARLY WORK

Ong's first published work was an entry to the Golden Point Award competition in 2005 titled "(The First Good Story)"[4]. A short story about a writer who submits plagiarized entries to writing competitions on a regular basis using an imaginative variety of false names; it won third prize in its category. Unfortunately, her award was rescinded due to suspicions that it was not entirely original work.

Despite the allegations of plagiarism, however, Ong remained productive, publishing a novella, a short story, and an essay in the span of two years. Perhaps her most critically successful work, the farcical novella titled *The Inadequate Life of*

---

[4] Perhaps a reference to Macedonio's *The Museum of Eterna's Novel (The First Good Novel)*.

Wilson Wong features a student who struggles with his studies in the day while working on the perfect love potion at night. Having finally concocted the potion, he organizes a party to secretly administer it to the woman of his dreams—a former classmate who is soon to return to her native country. While receiving rejection after rejection, Wilson describes the history of his alchemical pursuits, detailing his numerous failed attempts in a monologue that is also a meditation on romance and time; the objectification of women and of love; narratives and narrativity; and identity and individuality.

When the party struggles to come together because "everyone has boyfriends or better things to do"[5], Wilson announces the cancellation of it repeatedly. It is clear that Wilson does not want to cancel the party. These repeated proclamations of cancellation are only attempts at registering his disappointment with his friends. This does not, however, succeed, because he cannot help but conceal the bitterness in each announcement with a veneer of courtesy. This is elaborated into a discourse of failure that dominates the latter half of the book.

In the final pages, the book takes an unexpectedly dark turn. On the night of "the inevitable party"[6], Wilson is informed

---

[5] Ong Hwee Teng, *The Inadequate Life of Wilson Wong* (Singapore: Idastradia Books, 2006), p. 30.
[6] *Wilson Wong*, p. 47.

that his romantic interest has taken ill and is thus unable to attend the party. A few weeks later, when she disappears "back to her native country, perhaps, or back to that invisible nothing"[7], Wilson, overtaken by despair, imbibes the love potion himself. His last words in the book are: "I've made a poison"[8]. It is unclear if this is meant literally or simply as a rhetorical device.

Wilson Wong outlines the fascination with erasure that would come to characterize Ong's entire body of work. Most notably, as Wilson contemplates the "vanishing act"[9] of his romantic interest, he contemplates if he can truly know where she has left, or even if she still exists, using a variation of Berkeley's famous tree in the forest. He asks, "Does it really matter where we have disappeared to when we already have? Can a person (or anything, for that matter) really disappear?"[10].

Similarly, Wilson's final act, to drink his self-concocted poison, is a form of suicide—whether literal or abstract—and is said to be what he "wants most of all"[11]. Wilson is tormented at this point, suggesting that he will "always leave marks"[12] on the world around him. Perhaps he means that he will always find

---

[7] *Wilson Wong*, p. 80.

[8] *Wilson Wong*, p. 88.

[9] *Wilson Wong*, p. 81.

[10] *Wilson Wong*, p. 85, original emphasis.

[11] *Wilson Wong*, p. 87.

[12] *Wilson Wong*, p. 87.

himself in love, or perhaps that his existence will never be truly wiped clean from reality, even in death; it is not simply his life that is inadequate, but also his death.

This obsession with erasure is coincident with Wilson's desire for a confrontation with the void. One example of this is the frequent exposition on courtesy in the novella. Courtesy for Wilson Wong is a pretence, a form of theatre, a "somethingness"[13] that enables people to conceal the void. For Wilson, the ease of accessing materiality—or the ease of pretence at access to materiality—disguises the underlying void and, indeed, removes us from it.

Ong's next work was the short story "(The Last Good Story)", which eschews the humour and seemingly improvised nature of the novella for complexity in plot and a precision in prose. Published in the short-lived literary journal *Species and Spaces*, it is an experimental and highly unusual literary fantasy about a writer—presumably the last on earth—attempting to find permanence in a world where the old systems of signification are on the verge of extinction. One of its central questions—the authentication of existence—is encapsulated by the narrator's futile quest[14]. The story takes on an anachronistic bent—its format and language belong to a time past—as if to

---

[13] *Wilson Wong*, p. 15.

[14] Ong Hwee Teng, "(The Last Good Story)" in *Species and Spaces*, 1.2 (2007), pp. 42-3.

remind the reader of its confidence in the decay rather than the permanence of literature.

This fascination with time carries over to the startling essay that Ong produced in this period. Published independently and distributed at local independent bookstores, "The Flesh Eaters" is a meditation on death, writing, and romantic love positioned in between fiction and fact. The writing is allusive and references literature, philosophy, film, and music. Employing stereotypes that compare, individually, sleep ("To die, to sleep,/To sleep—perchance to dream"[15]) and writing ("The work is the death mask of its conception"[16]) to death, Ong repurposes these clichés in this essay to subvert common narratives of romance.

This essay exploits ambiguities between fiction and truth, a strategy that Ong would revisit later in her career. Considered relative to the trajectory of her work, however, it identifies an evolving approach to her thematic concerns that would come to define the second half of her bibliography.

---

[15] William Shakespeare, *Hamlet*, edited by A. R. Braunmuller (London: Penguin Books, 2001), 3.1.64-5.

[16] Walter Benjamin, "One-Way Street" in *Walter Benjamin: Selected Writings, vol. 1, 1913-1926*, edited by Marcus Bullock and Michael W. Jennings (Cambridge: Harvard University Press, 1996), p. 459.

THE TRILOGY

In Ong's early published work, we observe a fascination with erasure and cancellation premised upon failure. In the unusual trilogy that followed, Ong developed her ideas on the possibilities of erasure, while also exhibiting an inclination towards formal experimentation. I want to suggest that it is possible to see these efforts at experimentation as a shift in Ong's approach to literature.

Ong's trilogy is set in a fictional Singapore that may be called a fantasy of exaggeration. It is a Singapore in which tropes and archetypes come to life—the city is populated by heroes, villains, detectives, bohemians, wastrels, and poets. In this sense, it is not dissimilar from the work of other New Singaporean Literature writers, who have often resorted to a fantastic Singapore that Joanne Wee has dubbed the "infra-structural nation"[17].

The trilogy begins with the longest work by Ong, *Immolation*, a surrealistic novel which details the hunt for a scarred man suspected to be a serial murderer, whose marks are initially presented as attempts at self-erasure. The scarred man's battered body itself recalls the Beckettian body, unable to be reconciled with the abstraction of narrativization, a mark of

---

[17] "'There's No Art'", p. 41.

presence that cannot be erased, or indeed, flattened out by the act of storytelling. Indeed, there is a direct reference to Beckett in this variation of a line from *Texts for Nothing*[18]: "So I say to the body, Get up, get up now, and it struggles, like a bag of old bones, this sack of scars, foundering in the street"[19]. This is juxtaposed against the image of an infant at the end of the novel, its "generic body [is] clean and unscarred, almost as if it wasn't there"[20]. The body is in excess—that is, it exceeds the narrative—and, like the scars that it bears, cannot be erased.

Even as the scarred man appears to seek a direct form of cancellation, the formal features of *Immolation* suggest that Ong is pursuing more abstract avenues in her search of the possibility of disappearance. Specifically, she tests the potential for disappearance via the loss of meaning. For instance, the novel's unusual blend of genres—detective fiction, existentialist novel, essay, personal memoir, and so on—constitutes a rupture of categories that challenge the ability of genres to signal and signify.

---

[18] "I say to the body, Up with you now, and I can feel it struggling, like an old hack foundered in the street" from Samuel Beckett, "Texts for Nothing", translated by Samuel Beckett, *Stories and Texts for Nothing* (New York: Grove Press, 1967), p. 75.

[19] Ong Hwee Teng, *Immolation*, (Singapore: Scholastic Press, 2008), p. 55.

[20] *Immolation*, p. 304.

At the same time, the multiplicity of overlapping and conflicting "truths" in *Immolation* serves to attenuate meaning in the narrative. In *Immolation*, the narrator begins with an arguably well-defined profile, despite an ambiguity of purpose. He has had a bad childhood, is engaged in a long-term project to release all of the blood inherited from his alcoholic father, is jobless, and concerned about the murders. As the novel progresses, however, these stable truths are constantly tested, with the narrator ceaselessly adjusting his story, retelling and reframing earlier statements. By the end of the book, we are uncertain even of the narrator's gender. This diffraction of narratives is a diffusion of truths that contests the narrative's facility to contain meaning.

Another notable formal strategy employed by Ong in *Immolation* occurs throughout the book: Words, and later in the book, letters are scattered across several pages, at first seemingly randomly. In fact, these words form whole sentences that simply progress at a different pace, stretched to the point that they eventually become simply sounds. Dispersed and isolated from their original context, they lose their ability to retain their intended meaning. This "expansion of time"[21] is consistent with the scarred man's self-aware narrative, which constantly refers to the limitations of storytelling in its ability to accurately create a sense of time. I am reminded of Borges's

---

[21] *Immolation*, p. 129.

proposition that "in the novel the consecutive is more noticeable"[22]. Here, the consecutive is no longer noticeable, and the novel's—narrative's—capacity for meaning crumbles.

In her next work, a novella titled *The Gospel of Goose*, Ong continues to examine the idea of disappearance without resorting to erasure. *The Gospel of Goose* deals with a very literal iconoclast who is obsessed with destroying all icons and iconography. In contrast to the scarred figure of *Immolation*, this iconoclast—the titular Goose—seeks to erase his "symbolic existence"[23] rather than his physical body. Goose, a deranged narrator also haunted by an apocalyptic vision in his dreams, sees his iconoclasm as a resistance, a last stand against his "unending subjectivation"[24]. His unfortunate curse, of course, is that he cannot actually erase his so-called symbolic existence, and he ultimately accepts, in an echo of Blanchot, that even his death cannot be his own.

Goose eventually recognizes that the enterprise of cancellation is a futile one. Almost exactly in the literal middle of the novel, Goose realizes that he has to do the opposite—to relentlessly pursue his subjectivation—in order to disappear.

---

[22] Jorge Luis Borges, interview with Fernando Sorrentino in *Seven Conversations with Jorges Luis Borges*, translated by Clark M. Zlotchew (New York: Whitston Publishing Co., 1982), p. 128.

[23] Ong Hwee Teng, *The Gospel of Goose* (Singapore: Idastradia Books, 2009), p. 5.

[24] *The Gospel of Goose*, p. 20.

This explicates the double bind of erasure in which freedom is coupled with a loss of identity.

Goose's frequent and often slightly inaccurate use of the expression "better late than never" and his use of various idioms in a casual and banal fashion constitute a strategy of linguistic repetition that reinforce the failure of meaning. In the world of Ong's trilogy, where even expressions with the most stable and seemingly well-defined of meanings become whitewashed into meaningless sounds, one disappears not into emptiness but into noise. This is the premise at the heart of Goose's apocalyptic dreams, that in the event of gross excess, discernibility and contrast become non-existent, and existence becomes imperceptible, and therefore nullified.

Thus, Goose's use of idioms—expressions which may be said to be relatively stable in meaning—causes them to lose their distinctiveness, expressive power, and ultimately their meaning. The words—scars on paper bodies, marks on reality— are not so much erased (as they are inerasable); instead are dispossessed of meaning and influence, lost in a sea of equally meaningless words and phrases, vanishing. Unlike Beckett, Goose tests the possibility of the void not in the use of silence, but in a sea of noise. If "[t]he words outlive me, because in a certain sense my existence is irrelevant to them"[25], nothing survives when the words turn to noise.

The Cancellations forms the last third of this unusual trilogy. A poem of 189 words in seventeen lines, it is an ambiguous piece describing an assortment of villains of literature. One of them, for instance, is a murderer of characters, whereas another secretly adjusts the meanings of words and alters reality much in the way a time traveller might by changing the past. Featuring numerous allusions, a generous number of puns, and the prominent use of slant rhyme, *The Cancellations* challenges the sufficiency of words as vectors of meaning. It is a brief record of a literary, linguistic, and semiotic history that exposes the realm of possibilities as a history of the nothing-there, the never-has-been and never-will-be—the vacant tragedy of our narrated lives.

A SECRET LITERATURE

The last of Ong's published work (so far, one hopes) is *A Secret Literature*. Independently released on sheets of A5 paper stapled together, all known copies of *A Secret Literature* were placed in a stack housed in a box at one exit of Bishan, Ang Mo

---

[25] Ullrich Haase and William Large, *Maurice Blanchot* (London: Routledge, 2001), p. 13.

Kio Park. Exposed to a variety of hazards—including the birds, rain, and harsh sunlight—every known copy of the text is significantly damaged (my own has turned brittle and yellow). Combined with the specific and unorthodox location of its distribution, *A Secret Literature*'s, arguably, unusual history as art installation emphasizes the temporal condition of the text[26].

The text itself is an ersatz essay, in which an academic grows increasingly frustrated over the course of the composition of an essay, with her inability to properly comment on the work of Shafiq Ishak. Shafiq Ishak is described as, most famously, the author of *Vanishing Man*, a novel about an illusionist who fails to reverse his vanishing effect, failing to bring a volunteer back onto the stage during a performance. As things rapidly get out of hand, the philosophical illusionist contemplates his own repertoire, magic history, the entertainment industry, theater and spectacle, and a variety of existential ideas, while being forced to take increasingly desperate measures as his livelihood and eventually his life come under threat.

In *A Secret Literature*, the academic—one Ong Hwee Teng—almost preposterously proposes that the various missing characters in Shafiq Ishak's work are in fact Shafiq himself. By

---

[26] The box containing the papers was removed by the police four days after the first reported sighting of it under the justification that it was a form of littering.

drawing upon her personal background and dramatizing the tension between the fictive and the real, Ong performs—through her academic persona—a number of fears that, unfortunately, I find familiar.

Ong's revisiting of the porous separation between fiction and truth suggests that there is always some truth in fiction, as much as there is always fiction in truth. Reality—a term which I admittedly use loosely in this paper—is not simply constantly narrated in the world according to Shafiq Ishak (and one supposes the literature of Ong Hwee Teng as well), but constantly *fabricated*. For the tree in the forest to fall without anyone to hear it, it is first necessary to invent the plant, the forest, and the sound of falling trees. The academic's great fear is not simply the possibility that she will not be believed, but also the way in which it reflects on her own falseness as fabrication and fiction.

Ong's academic persona explicates this fear by using the fictional words of Shafiq Ishak, who declares: "Everything I write instantly becomes fictions"[27]. Indeed, while Barthes's *effet de réel* suggests that more often than not texts incorporate formal features that provide the impression of reality, this document encounters not the inevitable weight of the truth, but the pressure of fiction. That is to say, in the process of

---

[27] Ong Hwee Teng, *A Secret Literature* (Singapore: Self-published, 2010), p. 3.

explaining the truth, Ong's academic inevitably is complicit in the process of its fictionalization.

This is what lies behind the academic's apparent sense of discomfort throughout the mock essay. She betrays a fear of making unfortunate puns and pompous declarations, and is also unusually repetitive, circling around the same propositions in a manner that is (for Ong the Author) uncharacteristically untidy.

Yet, such a reading of this text is based upon an understanding that it is easy, or even possible, to differentiate between Ong the Author and Ong the Academic Persona. This is Ong's final gambit, that the contestation over her real and fictionalized selves will smear boundaries and affect her authorial authority. Like Goose and the scarred man, Ong herself chooses the void by surrendering her ability to speak.

A Secret Literature

In Borges's "The Secret Miracle", Jaromir Hladík, sentenced to die by firing squad, asks God for an entire year to finish his play *The Enemies*. God grants him his wish, with the miracle year occurring in the time "between the command to fire and its execution"[28]. No one learns of this miracle (hence the title), and the play too remains a secret.

Ong's literary project—forgive my indulgence in terming it as such—is one in search of the possibilities of erasure. Ong's is a literature of effacement that seeks the void, echoing, of course, the Derridian/Heideggerian approach of *sous rature*. It is, if you will, a lit*erasure*, or—pardon the indulgence—a liter*asure*. By tracing the trajectory of Ong's development as an artist, we find an emphasis on the inadequacy of the form and the failure of the possibility of erasure in her earlier work. We can then understand the later emphases on thematic and formal approaches as an evolving strategy premised upon ideas of oversaturation and excess.

Ong Hwee Teng has faded from the public awareness since. Her books are no longer in print and some of her shorter works are permanently lost. Curiously, it seems even people extremely familiar with the local literary scene barely remember her name. Like Hladík, her work and her life has seemingly become little more than a story. Having rapidly fallen into obscurity, her biography has contributed to her secret literature.

In the 1983 film *WarGames*, the computer learns the concept of futility after analysing various scenarios of nuclear

---

[28] Jorge Luis Borges, "The Secret Miracle," translated by Anthony Kerrigan, *Ficciones* (New York: Alfred A. Knopf, 1993), p. 120.

war and famously concludes that "the only winning move is not to play"[29]. Like many of Ong's characters, however, it is too late for me now. Having already written the first word, I also acknowledge that I will never have the last.

"By believing passionately in something that still does not exist, we create it. The non-existent is whatever we have not sufficiently desired"[30]. This is the paradox that confronts me as I write these words. For someone who is for all intents and purposes non-existent, I can only hope that this account—this story—will leave its mark. Yet, it also participates in a project of fictionalization that protects her disappearance. I am at odds with the authority of my own voice. It is the only thing I have, and I despise it.

POST-SCRIPT

This paper was first drafted in July 2012. Since then, I have submitted the paper to a number of journals only to be rejected time after time. This submission, therefore, is something of a last resort—or perhaps a cry for help. I am uncertain if I should feel relief or despair that I cannot even put

---

[29] *WarGames*, directed by John Badham, United Artists, 1983.
[30] Nikos Kazantzakis, *Report to Greco*, translated by P. A. Bien (London: Faber and Faber Limited, 1973), p. 434.

my name on this manuscript. Someone will hear of this story even if it survives only as fiction. Are not all stories fiction after all?

In that time, I have also received a note from Ong, who must have acquired a copy of my work while I was circulating drafts among my friends. I have deliberated over the inclusion of its contents for a considerable amount of time for reasons that should be obvious to any reader of this paper. I have ultimately decided to reproduce the note. While my memory is not what it used to be, I have found it easy to recall and believe the following transcript to be accurate:

Dear [*name withheld*],

Do you like magic? Each magic trick has an initial state and a final state. Everything in between is the process, the trick itself. In many cases, there is nothing fantastic about the initial or the final states. A vanishing act begins with a person's being there and ends with a nothingness. The magic is in the act, in the process, in change, in time, in memory.

As you well know, an act of disappearance is premised on the event of appearance. The word itself is a negation. This makes the ideal disappearance impossible, because every possible erasure is marked.

The perfect effacement is undetectable. The only way to disappear completely is to erase the word itself.

When we are born—even before we are born—we make an imprint on the world around us. We add to this imprint as we grow and decay. Every single thing we do and don't is another branch on this spider's web. The reason we do not acknowledge the threads left by so many around us is because there are so many of them, and so much sameness. I have done all I can to hide my imprint. I have exploited its condition to my purpose. It is all I can do.

When I was a child, I was once accused of littering. I was in the National Stadium with the rest of my class waiting for a preview of the National Day Parade to begin. A teacher spotted a piece of litter near where I was sitting and did not hesitate to reproach me for it. I tried to explain that she was mistaken but I only made things worse. Every attempt at explanation was interpreted as defensiveness or barefaced denial, much as in that Chinese saying.

You face the same problem. We all do. The more we speak, the further we project ourselves away from the authentic, or the true, or the truth. I'm not sure anymore. But people don't remember. "No, they forget and retain nothing in forgetting"[31]. They disremember. Having relinquished my ability to speak, I am lost to oblivion, and glad that I am.

I appreciate your effort to remember me, and to keep me remembered. While it is contrary to my efforts at writing my-self into the silence, it also draws an immaterial connection between the two of us. The void can get lonely. I am human after all. I'm afraid for you. This will only intensify your sense of the unreal because the real is derived from the inventions of others. Remember this: It's not so different from the plight of most people, who are stories and songs and fictions.

Cancel everything,

HT

Dec 2012

I feel that I should be more surprised than I really am at having lost the note. I did not compose it.

---

[31] Maurice Blanchot, *Awaiting oblivion*, translated by John Gregg (Nebraska: University of Nebraska Press, 1997), p. 31.

Seven Failures by Peter Lai: An Exhibition Guide

About the Artist

Peter Lai (b. 1954) is a multidisciplinary London-based artist who was born in Kuching, Sarawak. His family moved to Taiwan and then Singapore during his childhood. For several years, his arts practice was primarily based in Singapore as well. Despite these connections, however, Lai's work has gone relatively unheralded in Asia, and this is only the fifth time that Lai has exhibited in Singapore in a career spanning four decades.

In fact, this is the first substantial presentation of his work in Singapore in over two decades. After his controversial performance piece *Stolen Virtues* in 1995, Lai maintained a low profile for several years, only re-emerging in 2004 with a video art series in London. He has received more substantial attention over the past five years with renewed interest in the artists of his generation, including Valerie Tang and Suleiman Ibrahim.

Family

At the beginning of this exhibition is the installation titled *Family*. While not part of the *Seven Failures* series, this has been included as a valuable introduction to the artist, given both its thematic focus on failure and disenfranchisement, and demonstration of Lai's penchant for blending fact and fiction.

Family is presented here for the very first time despite having been conceptualized in 1996. One reason for this long interval is its difficult subject matter. The piece openly deals with the falling out between the artist and his siblings over what is alleged to be Lai's sister's association with the convicted cult leader David Poon.

Featuring a large metal frame containing various personal artefacts dangling from above, suspended using fishing line, the piece also includes an audio component, recordings of Peter Lai reading what are presumably words exchanged between the siblings. Viewers step into the space and interact with the physical items, which distorts the audio recordings. The noise of the hall is also continually recorded and fed into the sound projections, eventually putting the initial state of the piece out of reach. Paired with the out-of-context physical objects contained within, it suggests the gradual decay of truth and good intentions, much like the deterioration of familial relationships, if not relationships in general.

With its very public airing of dirty laundry, the piece was always going to prove challenging to exhibit. Lai was at first adamant but gave up upon being threatened with a lawsuit by his sister when the concept was allegedly leaked. Another reason it failed to be realized is that the vast amounts of data and on-the-fly processing would have rendered this a technologically unfeasible installation at the time of its conception.

Lai suspected that he would die before seeing a successful installation (*The Straits Times*, 2 April 1996), although this has proven false. This installation has been completed by visual artist Sarah Dragon and musician Benny Chan and replaces the audio recordings with fictional lines from an imagined family dispute.

That incorrect prediction is but one failure in an assemblage of failures. At its heart is the story of a failure of a family. The incompleteness in being unable to use the original audio recordings is another. Most of all, by completing this piece, it performs the erasure and irretrievability that is its subject, with stories and subjective experiences taking the place of what had truly unfolded: exchanges, thoughts, and emotions, now lost like the innocence of childhood.

Seven Failures by Peter Lai

On the surface, *Seven Failures by Peter Lai* is an exhibition that introduces seven of the artist's unsuccessful attempts at adapting a Singaporean play—Kuo Pao Kun's *Descendants of the Eunuch Admiral*, first staged in 1995. However, the series as a whole may also be taken to as a single text, a piece of installation art that thematizes and narrates this failure. Within its narrative, Lai is described as a reclusive artist who developed dozens of such attempts over a period of years. The exhibition features various items relating to seven of these failed attempts. In detail, these attempts at adaptation and the ways in which they are represented in the exhibition are:

1. *#2: nothings/nowhere/neuters*: A series of photographic prints tracing the narrative of *Descendants of the Eunuch Admiral* without language. All prints are exhibited here.

2. *#9: Ghost Games*: A projection of archival footage relating to the play featuring elements of randomization introduced by an interactive computer platform. The full piece is included here.

3. *#13: Sun Kid*: A performance art piece represented in the exhibition by handwritten notes and a script. Visitors were encouraged to become temporary sculptures by following instructions.

4. *#32: Echo Station*: An installation featuring a large metal frame, reproduced here. Excerpts from the source text are suspended by string from the frame's ceiling. Participants were encouraged to take these excerpts, and each act of removal distorted the soundtrack playing within the room. At the end of the exhibition, participants who left their addresses were mailed a copy of the recorded soundtrack.

5. *#33: Leaving, traces.*: An island-wide project utilizing the same metal frame described in the previous project. In the original presentation, a number of USB flash drives were hidden across Singapore with instructions to return them to the location where the frame was installed. This project is described in the exhibition, with items such as the flash drives, design sketches, and notes on display.

6. *#37: (Untitled)*: A singular artefact produced after the death of his sister, this project is a type of scrapbook chronicling Lai's struggles during this period and frames his attempts at adaptation within the context of mourning. Only fragments from the original piece have survived, which are featured here.

7. *#45: Volleyball*: A series of mutilated volleyballs, often resembling faces, a number of which are collected in this exhibition.

In all, *Seven Failures by Peter Lai* tells the story of a man struggling with both personal challenges and the inability to fully resolve feelings of indebtedness, anxiety, and displacement. It presents Lai as an artist in search of authenticity, idealistic but neurotic, constantly second-guessing his roles as interpreter, translator, and author. Resonating with the thematic features of the source text, it explores topics of performance and spectrality, cultural memory and inheritance, and the interrelation between art and life.

Significance of Work

On the surface, this piece is a distinctive take on *Descendants of the Eunuch Admiral*, performatively presenting the processes of adaptation, interpretation, and memory. While Kuo has been feted by critics and canonized in Singaporean literature, this project examines such acts of canonization and interrogates the idea of an artistic legacy. Positing Kuo's *Descendants*—and indeed his entire body of work—as a type of cultural inheritance, it builds on themes already present within the original play to develop questions about literature and culture in Singapore. Couched between text and performance, *Seven Failures* tests both the limits and possibilities of how texts can be remembered, performed, and made anew.

At the same time, the work—perched somewhere between fact and fiction, exhibition and adaptation, biography and autobiography—uses its indeterminate state to reveal an uncertainty at its core. Contrary to the romanticized failure so common in artistic discourse, *Seven Failures* is a fragmentary portrait, obsessive but vulnerable, determined but tentative, almost listless.

This should come as no surprise. Perhaps because of his childhood, Lai's body of work has long been framed by the themes of dislocation and disconnection, and *Descendants of the Eunuch Admiral* represents the perfect platform for these obsessions. Desolate and wonderfully strange, the original play traces the life of Admiral Zheng He in his voyages of discovery in fantastical fashion through motifs of cultural rootlessness, displacement, and castration—the last of which is also the primary thematic feature of Lai's last major work in Singapore, *Stolen Virtues*.

Apart from thematic concordances, however, the absence of both author and admiral coincides with Lai's private life. We can read into the presentation of these failures and their details a type of personal mourning that encroaches into public space. Apart from losing his sister to illness, Lai's brother took his own life in 1995 in a controversial case allegedly related to the irresponsible use of family details in the *Stolen Virtues* performance. Such unsavoury particulars might not typically belong in an introduction like this, but here they reveal the politicization of identity at the heart of *Seven Failures*.

Ultimately, it is a performance of disembodied guilt, a picture of regret, displacement, rootlessness; a portrait of atonement coloured by a profound impossibility; a letter with neither origin nor destination.

The Tain

I

Looking back now, this is clearly your masterpiece.

You've seen it so many times. You play it at least once a night while holding onto this wooden box in your hands. On a CRT TV, on a flatscreen, on a projector, through VHS, VCD, and DVD. Nowadays, you just watch it from a computer, easily looped, the electric glow of the screen like the harsh light of day. It's a ritual. You've done this every night since the film's release. You've cycled through every version that's ever been released, and even some that have never been. The shots scroll through the familiar opening montage of stylishly dressed men and close-ups on fake American money, counterfeits, and criminals.

There it is, that scene from *A Better Tomorrow*, Mark Gor setting one of the notes and lighting a cigarette with the fire. He does so partly to show off that money has a different meaning to him now. He's rolling in it. What's such a little bit of cash to a high roller like him? He's also doing so because none of this is money. It technically has no value, except for what we ascribe to it, but isn't the same true of all money?

You see the fire reflected in the shades, the warm glow illuminating Chow Yun Fat's famous face. You can't exactly say why you do this every night, why you watch and rewatch this scene of glorified criminal activity. The simplest explanation is that you're proud of your work. You are, after all, the prop man who created the prop money. Some might call it nostalgia, but what's wrong with a little pride in your efforts? There is also a mournful aspect to this. This film is a document, capturing the moment in which the prop money passes into a kind of afterlife, but also into the reality of the world. It is a moment you cannot return to, and what is nostalgia but the impossibility of return?

You hear noises outside. It's your son. He's just come home. You live in this dingy flat together. There's too little personal space and too much history contained in this home. It's become quieter since your wife passed. Since her death, you and your son have grown ever more distant. He has become involved more and more with community activities—volunteers with the local bookstores and such. Which is good. At his age, he needs what friends he can get.

You tap on the wooden box anxiously. You won't go out to greet him. Earlier today you had an argument that was pointless and nonsensical, as all arguments are at this stage in your life. You don't remember how it had started, but it was probably something mundane that opened the floodgates for accumulated grievances. That's just the way it goes. You're probably not speaking to each other for the next couple of days, but none of this is out of the ordinary. Give it time. Things will be fine again.

He doesn't understand this at all. To him, you are a relic from a bygone era. It's not worth the time or energy to learn more about your world. You remember the mildly annoyed look on his face as you asked him if he could help you with digitizing some of your old copies of the film. You don't blame him. Who in their right mind would see any value in these old films? Besides, he's more interested in the literary arts. He wants to become a writer, a novelist, he says. He wants to create something permanent, something that will outlast the vicissitudes of time, a tower in the tyrant sea. A very Joycean ambition, one that he has clung onto blindly for twenty or thirty years. He's now middle-aged and he has nothing to show for it.

He doesn't yet understand that there are two ways things survive: as monument and as ghost. You're not sure he even understands the film. The times have changed. These are the days of upfront resistance and explosive violence. He does not quite see the same anxiety that you all bore, does not see that all of this was a resistance against the vapidity and viciousness of a superficial reality. Most of all, despite the twenty or thirty years he has put into his writing, he does not yet understand that craft is the path through which one finds mastery of self and unmasks the illusion of reality.

You can still do it. You can still create prop money as well as you ever have. You look at your hands, now old and wrinkled. Spots have blossomed across the skin, and your knuckles have turned into tangled knots resembling tree roots. Arthritis has robbed you of the dexterity, the freedom of movement, but all you need is more time. Your craft is one built on patience and detail, not excessive showmanship or transient performance. It's the thing itself that is transient, taking on a life after its completion, telling its own lie, slowly transitioning into the sea of reality.

The best props don't call attention to themselves—they simply blend in. Aged paper, false ice cubes, invented ads on fictional newspapers, and quiet cellophane. They are forgeries of the highest order. Forgery is a Chinese art. Zhang Daqian was revered for his ability to reproduce paintings with great skill. And we learn calligraphy by first imitating the masters. It is a method of inheritance, almost genetic in nature. It is also a means through which to test the nature of our semiotic existence.

In fact, all forgery is a method of questioning the world. Mark Gor may not realize it, but counterfeiting currency is an anarchic resistance against the principles of economy. After all, it is the incineration of value. He lets his greed cloud his vision. He's always compromised, which leads to his eventual death in the film. He would of course return in sequels like some kind of restless spirit. It is true what they say, cinema is the art of ghosts.

Ironically, filmmaking is the ultimate capitalist venture. At least for the most part. Not only are the productions themselves investments of millions of dollars and the entire economy of cinema built around box office success, the industry itself is a comprehensive system of labour exploitation.

Decades after this film, the people behind another movie, *Trivisa*, would get into a bit of a scandal over prop money. Maligned for being too good at their jobs . . . Preposterous. There's no such thing as being too good at the art of forgery. People don't understand the concept of illusion. Ultimately, all art aspires to be invisible, to be undetectable in its artifice. The whole point, of this art at least, is to disappear, to be brought into a new kind of life and in doing so dissolve into nothingness.

You take great pride in your work. This prop money represents a kind of pinnacle. Four times as false, as prop, as fiction, as counterfeit, and as counterfeit of a counterfeit. How will this possibly be exceeded? You don't know. You've never found the answer in all the nights staring at these moving images.

You briefly wonder if you could explain this to your son—that your obsession with this excerpt of film is an artistic ambition, that your life's work was built upon an aspiration to approach the old masters. Would it get the two of you talking again? Would it finally lend some substance to a relationship that has become increasingly empty of participation? Perhaps, but you don't know if you know how to be this vulnerable in front of anyone. You know only that you look like an old fogey revelling in past glories, like a bug trapped indoors, charging towards the glass repeatedly, desperately seeking the sun.

You start to panic, wondering if this is it. Maybe this is the moment that you and your son will never speak again. Have you unwittingly reached the point of no return? Have you crossed that invisible line that has closed all other futures? A powerful feeling grips your heart. The feeling of destiny, as though drawn closer to death.

You open the box. Around you, flaking wall paint, moss-covered books, and the creaking whirl of the electric fan. The loud sounds of night traffic filtering through the windows. The glow of city lights. And as you peer into the box, you see it, pristine as always, a banknote just like the one on screen, one last memento you've kept from a more glorious time.

Its destiny is to be set on fire. That is true of all of us. Our destiny is to burn out like the stars, might as well embrace it. You look again at the machine, see Fat Gor's visage immortalized in bits and bytes, a different kind of fire, looping and looping, living forever. You take out the cheap plastic lighter from your shirt pocket and think, if you complete this circle, if you let the note fulfil its purpose, will you finally complete your story too? Will your son stop treating you as an inconvenience, or worse, a trope of an elderly man? Will he see you again for the person that you are?

You strike up a light and, hands quivering, raise the prop note towards it. It is traditional to burn hell money as offerings to the departed. And this too is an offering, not to spirits, but to the memory of a life long dead, and the hope of an unknowable future. All art is an offering to that which is unknown. All art is a cry for hope.

You set it on fire, become mesmerized by the twirl of the flames. As the fire grows, you feel the heat approaching your fingers. It burns faster than you had imagined. You watch as the ash falls slowly onto tiled floor. You imagine your son seeing all of this, watching as the prop completes its path, fading into the realm of perfect sign, devoid of substance, possessed by symbolism. You imagine him seeing you chart a journey towards such invisibility too. Will you ever be so imperceptibly reabsorbed into his life again?

The ash collects in a scattered patch on the ground. Your fingertips suffer minor burns. There is a stinging in your hand. A warm breeze blows into the room. The perfect art.

II

Here's Godzilla! King of the nuclear wasteland!

Here's Godzilla! Roar, roar! Iconic sound effect.

Here's Godzilla! Rampaging through the cardboard city!

Here's Godzilla! Nothing but a 100-kilo suit. Hot as hell!

Here's Godzilla! Brave Nakajima Haruo, who moved like a bear.

Here's Godzilla! Sometimes villain. Enemy of humanity!

Here's Godzilla! Sometimes hero. Friend of children!

Here's Godzilla! Except you can't see him yet. You'll have to wait for the CGI.

Here's Godzilla on holiday! Hanging out on a deckchair, catching some sun. Is Godzilla cold-blooded? Hard to say!

Here's Godzilla at church! Seeking forgiveness, seeking salvation. They just make me kill, and kill, and kill, and . . .

Here's Godzilla, taking a poop! I mean, a creature so big has got to take a dump from time to time, right?

Here's Godzilla! Symbol of environmental crises or irresponsible nuclear research. Metaphor for untameable nature. Shorthand for humans are rubbish.

Here's Godzilla in my childhood imagination! Vanquishing evil kaiju, some kind of pet, some kind of friend.

Here's Godzilla at a restaurant! What does he eat?

Here's Godzilla in front of the bathroom mirror! He's thinking about why humans built Mechagodzilla, not just once but five times. Is there something wrong with me? Am I not good enough for you?

Here's Godzilla! On a weekend hangout with his pals Anguirus and Biollante. Shooting the shit.

Here's Godzilla, falling in love! Oh wait, it's not that kind of story!

Here's Godzilla in a retirement home! Just kidding! If only I could retire.

Here's Godzilla the eternal! Outlasting kings and prime ministers. Kept alive by box office capitalism.

Here's Godzilla in the Criterion Collection! Respect anew!

Here's Godzilla, lifeless corpse! Inject new life into it, Mr. Anno!

Here's Godzilla! Yes, it's me!

Here's Godzilla! Hello! It's me. I'm that monster. King of Monsters!

Here's Godzilla! I'll be anything you want me to be!

Here's Godzilla. Yes, Godzilla. Yes, that monster. Can I speak now?

   Can I speak?

I'll be anything

    you want me to be

III

The glow from the rectangle has started to wane. The music still flows in crests and troughs. Words scroll from the bottom to the top. Those are the names of the co-conspirators who came together to collaboratively fashion this lie.

He's seen this film before. He's seen all the other films too. At first, it didn't make sense to him why they would get anyone to pretend to be him. In fact, he was furious the first time he saw a portrayal of himself in a film. But he has stopped resisting, relented, become resigned. As with all things in the afterlife, everything fades into the deep grey of forever.

Ip Man sits contemplating what he has learnt in this age of cinema. Reading into these fictions has revealed facets of himself that he did not know before, but he wonders if this is more a matter of applying his subjectivity to what is essentially an unchanging creation. After all, cinema, he has realized, is but an illuminated ghost, an image that recurs and recurs with no hope of exceeding its original shape, a fraction of a reality with no future of its own.

He has seen himself played by four or five different actors, and still, it remains somewhat uncomfortable. While he has gradually come to terms with the idea that he has become a major film franchise, each time the screen comes alive, it still feels like an out-of-body experience. Despite effectively communicating the physicality of martial arts, cinema remains immaterial. He remembers what the practice of Wing Chun was like. A bodily art—one that is out of reach for him now—but also linked so intrinsically to the aspect of the mind.

He steps out of the building. As the rain descends on the old theatre, he thinks he will never get used to the way the rain travels through the boundaries of his tenuous physical presence. The soft patter of the raindrops comforts. He turns back and gazes at the building, in which the luminous machine whirs— an engine of fictions and truths, an interplay of memories true and false—ghosts producing ghosts.

Tomorrow is another day. He will be here again, watching, remembering, forgetting—watched, remembered, forgotten.

IV

Every day I go into the video store and leave a small note in a DVD jewel case or VHS sleeve of a movie I've seen. The note is no larger than my thumb, with a single word (always different) and initials (always the same).

I like to imagine stories to the movies I've watched. The life stories of crew members. Amusing, apocryphal anecdotes from the productions of famous films. Completely fictional easter eggs. The afterlife of characters. The notes reference these tales in my head but never tell them. That's not the point.

The store doesn't have much longer. It's no secret that everything will turn digital sooner or later. The man at the counter hasn't slept in weeks. The movies are years old. The floor has the smell of death. Nothing digital ever sleep, ages, or smells.

I never rent the videos that I insert the notes into. I don't want to be that transparent. Instead, I chart a path through the volumes, a trace of my subjectivity, an insistence that I was there once. I go to check the notes every two weeks or so. They usually vanish within a month, certainly within two. I wonder if they've fallen out, been cleaned up, or if there is a collector out there, someone who has archived them and found the shape of me.

Dark Matter

I had never been more delighted to have received a rejection.

One evening in August I picked up a large envelope from my mailbox. It was easy to tell that it contained a sizeable stack of paper, and I guessed quite correctly that it was a manuscript for a novel. I had been working on a number of writing projects at that time and I felt confident that one of them had come back in the mail accompanied by yet another rejection. I had, after all, amassed quite a collection of rejections over the years. I went over the rejection letter over and over again. The message was not dissimilar to those contained in the majority of rejection letters, implying some degree of regret and offering a sincere apology. Years of experience with such messages told me to expect to feel insulted, hurt, or disappointed—or some combination of these emotions. Instead, there was this abnormal joy. This joy was short-lived, quickly turning into confusion. It took me a while, but I finally realized what I was looking at. I was named as the author of both, though I hadn't written either, the cover letter or the manuscript. It was some kind of forgery, a fake, a fiction of a sort.

Uncanny. I felt as if I'd seen a ghost. Hurriedly, I checked everything. I reread the rejection letter, double checked that it had my name on it. I attempted to confirm that the mailing address was mine, shortly before realizing that it had to be since it came through the mail. There was almost no indication the publisher from which it had come back. I flipped through the manuscript, but it told me nothing new. Then, I read the cover letter again. I started from the end (it is often easiest to do so) and saw that it was indeed my name and my signature. Checking each sentence carefully, I also found that it very much resembled my own writing in terms of sentence structure and vocabulary.

I assumed the worst, my bewilderment quickly giving way to paranoia. Even if the mind generally does not prefer one, there was every possibility that a more ordinary explanation was behind it all. For example, it was perfectly plausible that I had in fact sent the submission out and had forgotten all about it. Perhaps the trauma of writing such a terrible novel had caused me to forget it.

I examined the manuscript. I spent hours and hours scrutinizing it, in search of clues to my impostor's identity. Titled *The River*, it featured about seven characters and a cockamamie plot. I actually enjoyed my first time reading it because of how absurd it was.

The River told the story of a pair of star-crossed teenage lovers, taking place in a fairly fantastical Singapore with its own version of the mafia. Its two lead characters were university students, Raman and Joyce, who, under extremely unlikely circumstances, had fallen in love with one another. The two of them had troublesome fathers who got in the way of their romance, because that's what fathers were made to do. Joyce's abusive father would commit two violent crimes as the story unfolded. Raman's father, on the other hand, was a dangerous man who had a very impressive and well-decorated career in the criminal underworld, and he wasn't very keen on seeing the two of them together.

This melodramatic mess was narrated by Joyce. The writing was fairly convincing as far as it created a relatable character caught in the middle of absurd developments. She quoted from canonical literature frequently, in a type of showy, self-indulgent way that somehow helped her characterization as a teenager. Even if the plot was riddled with holes, I found myself rooting for her as she went about her day, feeding stray cats, struggling with exams, recording her dreams, and fleeing from the local mob.

It wasn't a good novel. I was at first hopeful that the manuscript would be of some merit as it would have made things much simpler. I would be able to relinquish my own life, to just leave him—this other me—to it. That is, I would simply be able to disappear. Still, it wasn't the worst thing I had ever read. Besides, I had written much worse before.

But the quality of the novel didn't have much bearing on my response to it. Immediately after I finished reading it the first time, I started writing furiously. Confronted with the possibility that there was someone out there readily assuming my identity, to take my name, there was the naïve hope that a textual account would help me clear my name should the impostor do something illegal. Perhaps there was also an element of catharsis in writing, a way of dealing with the fact. Surely it wasn't every day that one was confronted by the prospect of a simulacrum. Soon, however, I realized that the writing was going nowhere. I stopped and took stock: There was the cover letter, limited information about the publisher from the rejection letter, and the manuscript itself. Those encompassed all of the clues I had about my impostor.

I found the term disturbing. Why did I keep referring to him as my impostor? Yet, what other name would I have for him? Namefake. Impersona. Falter ego. Should I even be allowed to name him? Perhaps I was the one infringing upon his life. Perhaps I was the fake. I had never wanted to impose on anyone, much less as an imitation. Had I inadvertently become a thief? Maybe I had been writing not in the hope of repossession, but rather to claim what was never mine to begin with. Ideas and identity. A sad shape hanging onto a counterfeit life.

In certain traditions, sightings of doppelgangers bring bad luck or foretell one's death. The years, however, have seen to the dilution of this belief. Still, I had long thought that it would be a terrifying thing, the encounter with one's spitting image. Perhaps it emerged from the simple fear of seeing oneself. I never kept photographs of myself. I didn't even have a mirror. And yet, even then, I felt the fear this fear of the uncanny.

I decided to solicit Joanne. She was familiar with my writing. I handed a copy of the manuscript to her and asked for her opinion, pretending that someone else had written it, even though someone else *had* written it. We went to a nice Korean restaurant, although, come to think of it, that is irrelevant now. During dinner, we talked about *The River* in more detail and I eventually fessed up. I told her that I had received the manuscript a few days ago along with a rejection letter addressed to me. Of course she didn't believe me. She just thought that I was lying just to hide my embarrassment at having written the potential novel. I panicked, and in my panic, summoned all the earnestness that I could muster in a naïve attempt to convince her that it was all truth. In my mind, I kept asking: What do I have to say for you to believe me?

Joanne gave me some advice, which I took, since she had never steered me wrong before. The game was on: I texted my friend Nicholas and asked him what he remembered of *The River*. He was the obvious choice because he was a good enough friend that he would put up with almost anything I threw at him, and he was also someone I might have shown my work to.

"Hey, do you remember the novel I wrote, *The River*?"

I waited anxiously for a reply the whole afternoon, like a defendant awaiting a verdict. I had no idea what he would say. Unable to hold my nerve, I eventually hid my phone under my pillow and decided to look at it again an hour later. Then I changed my mind and made it two hours later. Eventually, I stopped keeping track of the time. When I finally accepted the inevitability of the situation, I took my phone out, noticed that there was a message, and took a deep breath. I was scared, convinced that the world would have to be remade after reading the message, that it could no longer be the same.

There were two messages. I read the second one first since it was newer: "Think I still have the document. I can look for it."

My eyes drifted up. The first message: "Yeah, I quite liked it. My brother too."

I was shocked. Not just Nicholas, but his brother too? Surely there was no denying it now. I had for some reason forgotten about what I had written. Or perhaps I was making this doppelganger story up. Wasn't that what all writers did? Make up stories? I felt like Joyce, a person with no truth and no actuality, committed to stories, becoming stories. I was a charlatan exposed. Portrait of the artist as a young sham.

My mind raced in all directions. For instance, I started imagining that there was more than one impostor. This seemed unlikely because each new simulacrum only decreased the likelihood of us never finding out about one another. The implicit thought behind that was sinister, since it implied a degree of organization and conspiracy. I imagined these numerous selves going all about the country, all about the world, creating their own lives, but also one and the same life. The same face, the same name, the same voice, the same bones, each repetition producing its own effect, each performance a citation of an origin, at once consolidating its truth and substantiating its irretrievability. I wondered about family (do we have the same genes?), about friends (did we make the same friends?), and about enemies (I certainly hope we have the same enemies). I wondered if we fell in love the same way, and with the same people. Surely I must have done some really stupid things as my other selves.

After a week stuck in this state of bewilderment, I convinced myself that it was no way to spend the rest of my days.

I grew determined to forget all about it. I had to move on with my life. Life, of course, had other plans for me.

It happened three months ago, in November, when I was in the National Library, looking up something in Chinese. I had taken a bright red book from one of the shelves and was ready to make my way up the stairs when I heard a voice I thought I recognized. It was somewhat deep and unattractive. I went back towards the shelves and tried to locate the source. There was a mild sense of uneasiness that I couldn't shake. As I approached, I continued to rack my brains, attempting to connect it to a face. After a bit of careful tracking, I finally pinpointed the location of the voice. All I had to do was to step out from between the shelves and turn to my left. And then I realized that my uneasiness was easily explained: the voice was at once the most familiar and foreign to me. It was my own, disembodied and distant. I froze, staying hidden behind the books, unwilling to emerge. There he is, I thought. After all that had happened in three strange months, I had finally found him. Immediately I sank into despair. A wild terror arose within me. My head was pounding.

I turned and ran. Of course I ran.

I found myself back in my room not long after. It was as if the time in between had vanished. I didn't know what to do. The room felt cold. Sitting at a corner of my desk was the manuscript. Its substance seemed to offend me, its physicality—the materiality of the envelope, the pages, and the ink—all gruesome excess. Every such manuscript is the physical record of its history, and so *The River* was a story I should've known better than anyone else. But I didn't.

I wrote again, this time certain of what I was doing. I told this story, my story from the beginning over and over, in many different ways. I wrote with a black pen on a large notepad, in handwriting that was increasingly distorted. As I did so, I wanted to disappear into writing, to become writing. After all, we are all written in some way, just stories, just fictions. I was nothing more than one of these voices, or someone's story, or a relationship (relation: deferred, returning; from the Latin *relationem*: a bringing back). In real life, I shook hands with people, I ate food, I wrote with pen and paper, but I would always become memory eventually. Online, I inhabited a string in a world of bytes and vibrations, a ghost, an echo. In photographs, I was nothing but colours and angles. In writing, letters and letters, a voice in the dark, with no authentication and no hope for materialization. Everything only contributed to my own insubstantiality, this condition that belonged to everyone, our common ghostliness.

After a while, I realized that I had spent too much time worrying about a person who didn't exist. After all, what other possible explanation could there have been for that uncanny encounter in the library? I must have imagined him in my grave anxiety. Much as Joyce had conjured an expressionist Singapore in her narrative, perhaps my experiences were also in part some kind of fiction that I had concocted. Yes, I thought, that must have been it. There was never anyone in the library. A total fabrication. My anxieties slowly died away, until I reached a point where I could see how ridiculous I had been. I laughed at myself. I found myself smiling again. I just wanted to put it behind me.

Things never go according to plan. It happened as I was waiting for the train. I was standing among the faceless faces, near the end of the platform. I looked at the death-faces of the people around me, flattened, recoloured, frozen, transparent. There was a smell like the smell of bleach. I noticed the train coming in from my left. The people huddled closer together in anticipation. And then, as I was standing right at the door, he appeared. My double or my source. I must have looked as surprised as he did. He was inside the train, and I just stood staring through the window at my own face. I was quickly overtaken by my abject horror. All I could do was to run, trying to escape and yet knowing that it was all too late, that I was unable to pull myself away from some invisible path, some cosmic purpose that joined the two of us. I ran because I knew that I was, I am, I always will be a sham. Eventually, as the train departed, I slowed down, stopped, choking on my own breath. The lights around me appeared to dim. I felt that I was at the mercy of my double. I was the ghost, the insubstantial image in the mirror.

There was no denying it now. Once? Figment of my imagination. Twice? I knew there was no way. It was the last straw. Truth be told, I feared his guile, his ambition, his duplicity, and it was tempting to embrace nothingness, if I wasn't already nothing. I sensed danger even though I knew next to nothing about him. Someone out there was threatening to take away my person. It made me sick just thinking about it. He was claiming my life, all the things I had done, could have done, would have done. His existence alone meant that I could no longer fully be who I used to be. I could no longer talk about I, about myself. I had become a ghost clinging desperately onto my own dimming light, a shadow who owned no name, no voice, no material reality.

If my doppelganger was out there, I had to take the fight to him or risk losing everything that I had. I had to go to war because I needed to claim the start as my own. I had to be the original, the originator, and the origin. We may all be imitations of ourselves, but I needed to lay claim to the authentic performance. I had to lay claim to originality.

I didn't have a plan. I had almost nothing to go on. All I could do, I decided, was to stalk the places where I had seen him before. As soon as I could feel my legs again, I went home and cancelled appointments. I started making new plans on my calendar. The following Wednesday, I returned to the library. I brought along with me a camera, a bottle of water and a computer. With the computer as my disguise, I sat in surveillance. When it was dark, I went home. I didn't read anything, didn't watch anything on TV, didn't speak to anyone. Preparing for my next trip to the library was the only thing on my mind. Additionally, I went to the train station at the same time on the same day the very next week and stood at the same door. I repeated this pattern for four weeks to no avail.

The process was slow. I was wary of spending every day at the library initially. I didn't want it to overtake me, to totalize my life. I didn't realize then that it was already too late. Instead, I spent my time agonizing over pointless questions. Had he spotted me somehow? Was my plan a flop? Was it all some kind of devious trap? My obsession grew with my frustration. I spent less and less time at home, and before long, I was out each day trying to catch a glimpse of my double.

As it happened, my worries were unfounded. All I needed was a little patience. He appeared before too long, sitting alone at the library, seemingly at work on something, perhaps scheming to perpetuate this lie or plotting to destroy my life. Goosebumps. I was tempted to confront him immediately, but I knew that it would be pointless. I knew that now that I had him, I had to play the long game. When he left his seat, I sat down at the computer (we had the same face, and our clothes were relatively nondescript, so I hoped no one would notice), betting on the suspicion that we behaved in largely the same way, and that he kept a calendar in the same way that I did. Surprisingly quickly, I shook off the feeling that I was some kind of criminal and took pictures of his calendar with my phone. I left as quickly as I could.

Based on this calendar I went about following him, sometimes successfully and sometimes less so. I simply wanted to figure out what he was about. I learnt that we had many common interests. I followed him through museums and art galleries. I eavesdropped on his conversations and repeated his words. I walked the same paths, watched the same movies, ate the same food. I felt like his shadow, pursuing the same experiences vicariously. And yet, I was never really in any of those places. *I* was never *there*.

I tailed him nervously as he met up with my friend Nicholas, the very same. On a different day, he met up with Joanne. I wondered if they were all in on it, if it was some kind of bizarre conspiracy, but I decided that that was too absurd, and I couldn't think of any reason they would do so. Or perhaps I just couldn't stomach the thought. What was worrying, however, was that he had somehow found a way to reach my friends and they couldn't tell the difference. I had been replaced in their lives.

One evening, two months after I made a copy of his calendar, I managed to follow him home. I had failed to do so up until then because I would always lose sight of him somewhere, or I would lose my nerve. The building looked familiar at first, but the darkness of the evening delayed my recognition of it. It was my block. He was living in my flat. I didn't know how he got my keys. Besides, if he had truly been living in my place all the time, wouldn't we have met each other at some point in time? It was as if I had never really been home. Maybe I hadn't, I thought. After all, I had been sleeping poorly, if at all, and my memory wasn't to be trusted.

I left and returned, only to find no one home. Nervously, I spent the night in my flat, if it still belonged to me. In the week that followed, I would leave the house early in the morning and come back to it, only to find him emerging from the very same place and locking up the door. By this time, I had become accustomed to following him about undetected, and I would do so almost round the clock. He always returned home in the evening. I would take a bus, any bus, for fifteen minutes. Then I would take the same bus in the opposite direction and return home to find the flat empty.

I didn't understand how the space of my house worked. Confused and unnerved, I decided that it would be best for me to take the initiative and leave. I rented a place in the block just across from my place with whatever savings that I had. I also invested in a pair of binoculars. My new hideaway was completely bare apart from two chairs, a table, a refrigerator, and a bathroom. I had my computer and camera with me. I also bought large amounts of bottled water. Food was easily taken care of. I just bought an assortment of things that would keep initially, although in the end, it was too much trouble to think of something new each time. Eventually, I ate only bananas. They were easy to manage, and though they didn't keep for that long, it wasn't hard to keep myself stocked.

For money, I started taking up freelance writing jobs, using a pseudonym where a name was required. I spent the rest of my waking hours studying my impostor. I didn't call the police. I suppose I didn't know what I would tell them, and besides, I wasn't sure I could trust them to believe me. Of course, that was an admission that my claims of authority over my own life had dwindled, but it couldn't be helped.

One day, on a whim, I purchased a small circular mirror and set it aside in a corner of the room. If nothing else, it made the room seem a little less bare. At first, I couldn't bring myself to look into it, but I overcame this fear eventually. Perhaps it was because I had neglected sleep, or shaving, or my need for a haircut, but I couldn't help thinking that I was looking less and less like myself. I started to look at the mirror more and more, until it became a daily routine.

Even today, I look at the mirror frequently. It's become a ritual. It is somehow more interesting than that man living in my old flat. Perhaps it suffices that I have this mirror and in measuring how far it deviates from the memory of myself, I already understand what's going on in that other life. Indeed, now that I think of it, there is a certain flatness to his existence, as though the narrative of his life has already been prescribed.

Everything has become a ritual to me. I read *The River* over and over again each day, especially when he's not home, as though expecting some type of new discovery. I read the last pages repeatedly. The story ends in a suicide, of course, and it befits Joyce, who seeks to empty herself into the immateriality afforded to her by stories. I suppose that, in a way, I have achieved a similar state, a conjunction of the substance of stories and the nothingness of self. There is nothing left except the vacuum, and all vacuums invite intrusion.

I still eat bananas daily.

I write every day as well. Through my writing, I ponder some unanswerable questions. Has my face become his face? Have my words become his words? There is no point in thinking about these questions, except that they help me to mark time. I don't want to kill him. I don't even think I want my old life back. In a strange way, I think he depends on me, this negative presence, giving meaning to his life invisibly.

AFTERLIVES

The Fog

By the time my son forgot who I was, I had been dead for just 13 years. I suppose it was inevitable, but I had not expected it to happen so quickly and so soon. In retrospect, the signs had always been there, so perhaps it shouldn't have been surprising to me.

My name is Ong Kok Peng, although when I was 17, I also adopted the name Robert Ong. I am many things—an average teacher, a did-his-best husband, a mediocre father—but unfortunately, I am best known as a writer of fiction. I participated in the earliest editions of the Singapore Writers' Week, which would later become the Singapore Writers' Festival, when I had already become passé. In 1992, I was awarded the Singapore Literature Prize and then the Cultural Medallion in 2001. I had become canonized, and as I've learnt, canonization is a downward slope. A few years after, two of my novels—*The Fourth Erasure* and *Life and Times of Suleiman Ibrahim*—became compulsory texts for students. My most famous works are *The Fourth Erasure* and *Waterloo Street*. The first is about a woman who finds herself gradually disappearing after being unfairly dismissed from her job, while the latter chronicles the misadventures of a band of petty criminals trying to get by in rapidly modernizing Singapore. I was nominated as a professor of creative writing at the National University of Singapore in a short-lived attempt to mimic the creative writing programmes of the West. Despite the ill-fated programme, I was subsequently invited to speak at many events at the university.

These became the facts of my life as soon as I had died. They were the facts repeated at the funeral, in news articles, and certainly the everyday conversations. In my life, I was a writer of fiction and poetry of some renown. In my death, these things became the totality of me.

It's only when you become a spirit that you start to think about the physics of ghosts. For example, I have discovered that I cannot stray out of the house. There is something that keeps me here. A force. If I cross the front yard and take three steps out of the front gate, I am almost immediately engulfed by a bright fog, and unless I turn back, I can walk in that direction for what seems like forever. Yet as soon as I turn around, it is as though I haven't moved at all. Three steps back and I am in the house again. In the lesson of Orpheus, we learn that the conditions on the living are never to look back. Perhaps the condition of the spectre is to only be able to gaze backwards.

I haven't seen another ghost. I wonder if ghosts connect with one another, or if such community is even possible. I don't know if they meet up and make plans. Surely there is a limit to the plans we can make. Ghosts are creatures of the past with no possibility of a future.

The experience of death was not traumatic to my surprise. I died in my sleep next to the incomplete novel that I had been working on for the past seven years. The coroner declared an aneurysm the cause of death, even though I only learnt this a few years after the fact. It might have been painful—at least, the transition from mortal body to immaterial spectre—but I remember nothing of it. I was asleep one moment, and the next thing I remember, I was trying to understand why my legs seemed to be working properly again and how so much time had passed so suddenly.

Since then, I have also learnt that they cannot see me. That sitting there in the chair in the singlet, mindlessly scrolling through all the existent and non-existent television channels, is my son Andrew, who has spent the better part of his life attempting to emulate the literary success of his father. These days, he lives with his son Derek in our old house, spending his days staring blankly, sometimes scratching his feet. It is just the two of them in the house, and this ghost.

Andrew has Alzheimer's. It's in its early stages and has only been diagnosed recently, but such an affliction has an inevitability about it. That is, the ending seems predetermined, if it is not already unfolding. I regret most of all that he has wasted what could have been the most productive years of his life living in his father's shadow. He obtained a degree in aerospace engineering at a time when that was a popular discipline and the industry seemed to be on the up but promptly declared to his classmates and instructors that there was something else that he was truly passionate about. That is, he was determined to become a writer.

No parent ever wants their child to live in their shadow. I didn't even want him to follow in my footsteps. There is nothing particularly glorious or desirable about a writing career. It is a job like any job, and it almost never pays. But he has tried so hard to become a writer. I've attempted to help him along. I can hardly claim to be any good as writer, but I feel at least that I've walked the same path before and know a thing or two about the business. I gave him the name of other writers and editors, hoping that he would find some guidance in these connections, but he rejected all of these offers flatly, and even fell out with one editor when he learnt that I probably had a hand in getting them introduced. In fact, these rejections came so immediately I quickly understood that he wanted to find his own way. I suppose I should have been happy that he was striving to be independent, but there was a bitter energy about his pursuit of literary excellence, as though my own career had become a shackle for him.

Understandably, he refused to show me his work and instead grew intensely defensive about his career choice. I decided, in the end, that the only thing that I could offer was silence. I knew that he was too proud to take advice from his father and never spoke to him about it again. Of course I've been curious about his work. What sort of father wouldn't be? And one might assume that, as a spirit, I am perfectly capable of leafing through my son's incomplete writing. However, I believe in common decency. Besides, it is already oddly voyeuristic being invisible and all too able to pass through walls and doors. I fear that if I was to give myself to these indulgences, then these barriers no longer had any meaning to me, then there would truly be nothing human about me left.

I was lucky. I died before my mind deteriorated (although I suppose becoming an immaterial spectre is scarcely worth celebrating). I wonder what would happen if Andrew died with Alzheimer's. Would he too become a ghost? If he did, would he have his mental faculties at his disposal or would he be trapped in this dispiriting state of affairs? With fewer and fewer of his memories surviving, would life take on a different meaning? That is, would his suffering continue after the supposed release of death? As a father, as a human being, it pains me to watch him deteriorate in this fashion.

It began three or four years ago. One afternoon, he told his son that he was going out to buy some lunch and asked what my grandson wanted, only to forget that he had even asked twenty minutes later. In fact, he came home empty-handed, without even having lunch himself. At first an isolated incident, he repeated this lunch routine with worrying frequency within the span of a year.

Last year, he complained that there was a drop of blood on the study desk that would recur, reappearing each day at the break of dawn even if it had been cleaned, as though the house had been placed under some terrible curse. Derek, who was at the time just about to graduate from university, assured him that there was no such thing and went to great lengths to demonstrate that there was nothing there. Each time, Andrew insisted that he must have had it cleaned up already. Exasperated, Derek once told his father that his memory was not what it used to be. In a moment of startling lucidity, Andrew said, "How do you remember what you can't remember?"

At times, Andrew seems to remember me. He tells Derek of his youth spent in this house, how he ran through the halls, how he used to play hide-and-seek in the rooms upstairs. He tells Derek about the unique delight of finding the smell of beef rendang wafting through the house from the kitchen, and of the time his mother made him kneel in the hall for an entire evening for disobediently spending the afternoon at a friend's place. Sometimes, when he's alone, he hums a lullaby from his childhood, and it's as though he hears something in the echoes.

The property has been in the family for four generations. Most of the furniture here is older than my son. Some of it is older than I am. Andrew probably doesn't remember that the wooden bench he is now sitting on was partly crafted by his mother when she was 13. The family was friends with these craftsmen and my wife, Kim Neo, would spend time in their workshop on some afternoons. The craftsman, who were all middle-aged migrants from China, had arrived in Nanyang and settled in Melaka. My wife would spend many an afternoon there. Seeing that she was fascinated by the art, the craftsmen taught her for several months in an informal, wood carving apprenticeship. However, as the eldest child, the demands of supporting the family meant that she did not have much time for education—she dropped out of school soon after and began working—and much less for internships that did not guarantee employment. Plus, by that time, they had moved onto a scene featuring the Eight Immortals that was so clearly a bridge too far. She decided it was time to stop spending time in the workshop. Returning some fifteen years later, she would discover that the workshop had survived, that one of the old craftsmen was still there tending to his craft, and that this bench remained as though it had been retained just for this day.

She purchased it immediately even if it proved both financially and logistically challenging.

No one else knows this story, and with me this story too will fade. For there is no question that I will fade. I'm no physicist, but certainly, seeing as I do not have any conventional food intake and probably do not have the photosynthetic function of a plant, a ghost like me most likely manifests—with great difficulty—using some form of residual energy. Going by this theory, I have no doubt that my current existence will evaporate in due time. Where I go from there is uncertain. Perhaps I will fade into the ether. Perhaps I will go to Heaven or Hell. Perhaps I will reincarnate. I stopped giving thought to this a few months after I had turned into a spectre.

I still peek out of the windows, still watch the city change week by week, but this is the extent of my world, delimited by the walls of this house and the views from the windows. And those views are changing. I watch as skyscrapers are erected just three or four hundred metres away, as a newly completed wing of the nearby hospital encroaches into the space of my existence. With each new construction, each new inscription, the house's surroundings change, while it remains statically locked in the past.

I too am the same. Some days, the fog seeps into the door. Some days I can't even see what is outside. I am afraid that the dwindling of my son's mental faculties will also mark the end of my ghostly career. Ghosts are merely echoes, after all, and like all echoes, surely we will fade. My existence grows increasingly tenuous. Even if I persist—I keep imagining myself haunting these interiors, cycling through the same motions, repeating the same days. Isn't that what all hauntings are? Just memories and echoes. What happens when this house goes? Will I be freed, or will I no longer have anything to anchor me to the mortal earth? What happens when my son no longer knows the Robert Ong Kok Peng who once lived within these same walls? Will I become trapped here, little more than a collection of spectral effects?

These days, I look at my son from a distance. He looks so confused, so troubled. He looks as though he feels the weight of an entire life lived in his body, but his mind can find no trace of it. I look at him like I cannot find my son anymore. His spirit is gone. Exhausted voice. Dim eyes. A disarticulated spirit. I look at him like I used to, distanced. He has aged so much. He is so weak these days. Sometimes he struggles to stand, struggles to snap out of the daze that has possessed him. When he climbs the wooden staircase, the breathlessness is quickly audible. Life has become mechanical. It is about the breathing, about the aches, about the bodily dysfunction.

My son was born in 1958. He was a little underweight but was otherwise healthy. At first, his skin had such a deep blush it was almost purple, though this faded quickly. I was overcome with the thought that everything had fallen into place. The moment was fleeting, however. Fatherhood was not what I had expected. I had imagined that it would come somewhat naturally, and that it would bring the parents closer together. Neither of these proved true. Almost immediately, there was a gap that opened between us, a crevasse that only grew wider with the years. I remember sitting on that antique chair, the rosewood one with the dragons carved into the sides, looking as the toddler crawled across the floor. I did not know how to interact. I watched as he indulged in something called simple joy, or carefree innocence. It was something that I could never know. I realized then that I was not ready to be a father. Perhaps I was afraid that I would have such great authorship over someone else's life, that I could so comprehensively steer someone else's path, the responsibility magnified by the fact that he was my son. Perhaps I was intimidated by my inability to understand his language and the limits of his world. Or perhaps I was just afraid of such a young and joyous life.

The house creaks. It seems to be creaking more than it used to, as though it has developed a voice of its own over the decades.

In 1985, Andrew married Christine Tham, his classmate in university, after an on-and-off relationship over about five years. She gave me a good impression from the start, and initially I felt as though I could finally relinquish my fatherhood inadequacies to someone else. However, the challenges they had in their relationship soon became apparent and I wasn't optimistic about it. Their marriage was one of presumed necessity. At the time, I was fighting a cancer in my gut. Doctors were not optimistic about my chances and Andrew convinced himself that I was going to die. He also convinced himself that the thing I wanted most of all was to see him get married, when in fact—especially with the way that my marriage had turned out—I never really had any expectations. Also, I did not die. At least, not then. And so, the net result of this unfortunate debacle was a marriage that was more often difficult than it was happy.

The irony does not escape me. Here I am believing that my son's knowing me is the only reason I have persisted for so long, when at the crux of his troubled marriage was a failure to understand his father. However, my son is the only person alive who has been part of the life that I've lived, the only link to the layers beneath the veneer of the author. As Bob Dylan would have it, we each contain multitudes, but these multitudes are hidden, inaccessible, and inevitably lost. Over the past 13 years, my son has been the only person who remembers me like a real person, and I'm afraid that this will soon be coming to an end. As his memory decays with each passing day, I become more and more a ghost.

It was a Thursday afternoon when I decided to embrace my ghostly nature. I resisted for a long time because it felt like a final pronouncement of a sort, but one day, the inevitability of it all must have just overwhelmed me, and I have been haunting this house for the five years since. An old property like this cannot resist the tides of urban development. Over a century old, it is a bungalow built in a style perhaps typical of homes owned by especially well-to-do families in the late 1800s or early 1900s. Indeed, my father was a successful businessman who migrated from Xiamen to Nanyang at the age of 15. While not the most impressive specimen of such houses, I think we can all agree that it has certain historical value.

More interestingly, perhaps because of its gloomy façade, or the rumours about the eccentric family living within, it developed a bit of a spooky reputation over the years. Once, because of its history and the fact that it was still a handsome property, it was used as the main set for some television series on Channel 8 starring Li Nanxing. During filming, one of the set dressers complained about having an uneasy feeling whenever he went up the stairs. One of the bit actors also reportedly complained about having the same feeling throughout her time on set. She was not taken seriously until one of the supporting actors corroborated this. Some sources say that it caused a great disturbance that rippled through the cast and crew—as producers made calls to bomohs and Taoist priests—although other sources simply say that no one thought much about it and they went about their jobs professionally.

The tale of the single drop of blood that my son kept imagining, of course, only added to the myth of the haunted house. And so, my enterprising grandson had a flash of inspiration. Seeing that the place was falling into a state of disrepair, he turned this all into a business opportunity. To the livid objections of his father, Derek decided that turning the house into a museum of a sort, opening its doors to the public, was the best way of preserving it. It was jarringly marketed as both a historical building and a haunted house. Money would come in for restorations, and some manner of its history would also be preserved.

Like Andrew, I did not like the idea at first. Derek's intentions were good, but I became precious about the memory of my home. Even as academics researched the house, even as scholars volunteered to lead tours, how could it ever be possible to fully capture the memory of it without living it? The house would become a ghost of itself. Indeed, all aspects of it—the aesthetic experience, the architectural lineage, the emotional threads that have held it together all of these years—are trampled upon by the attempt to arrest it. None of these efforts convey the material basis of existence. None of these translate totally to *what it is*. It is a tale told over and over about that which used to be there. In time, all is eventually lost. But as time passed, I grew tired. Eventually, I gave up on the fool's hope that anyone would be able to see the house for what it was, or in fact, to see me for who I was.

When I had just realized that I had died, I considered just awaiting the instruction of some higher power to shepherd me to my next destination. However, I soon grew bored at simply waiting, particularly because there no longer was any meaning to any of the mortal habits and rituals. I felt my sense of purpose ebbing away. And then, something I can only call the urge to live took over. I wanted presence. I wanted to be remembered for who I was, to continue living in the memories of others. Three-dimensional. Substantial. Whole. The urge to live really is the promise of the future. I fought with all the stubbornness I could muster, but I didn't realize how difficult it would be, the meaninglessness of this existence like the hollowness of an echo. Each day, I feel the erasure, like a dense fog descending. Existing is exhausting.

As I gave up, I decided to support my grandson and to fully embrace the identity of a spectre. Admittedly, I was also convinced in part by the surprising success of the museum plan. As the doors opened, the house was no longer the home, but it welcomed visitors and ticket sales with quite some aplomb. When museum visitors and ghost hunters alike signed up for the night tours, I played my part. If I'm feeling generous, I make it worth their while, tickling Ouija boards and the scalps of overeager ghost hunters, tipping durable objects over and rocking chairs at random.

The truth is that the worlds of the living and the dead are so distantly divided that even the slightest manifestation takes a lot of energy. So, it is resignation. I doubt it will be long before this building is replaced by a new development project, and I have accepted it. That is the fate of most of these older, less spatially efficient houses. I have already said my goodbyes. But every so often, that urge to live, to carry on existing flickers, a mere glimmer, and in the deep grey drabness of the afterlife, I resolve to live again.

I hope you see now that this is a goodbye, but it is also a last stab in the dark. I am writing for the last time to keep something alive. I am a ghost, a luminous shape, a surface being, merely projection. There is no depth to me, no story underneath. I am the accolades I have won. I am the lessons I have taught. I am the photo that rests framed on the walls of this old house. That is not the way I want to go. What is the point of being falsely remembered? I want to be truly alive. Yet, I am a creature of data. I am all the information that I am. With nothing to be added, with no possibility of anything being added, all that awaits is true death. So I challenged myself to create again. I am only a memory, but a memory can be performed, interpreted, reimagined. Perhaps that will be life anew.

Every night, when the lights have gone off, I try to write more of this. It has taken me too long. I haven't written in a long time, and my materiality has limits. I write a little at a go. As I've mentioned, it takes great energy for a ghost to manifest any physical presence. And each night, when I am done, I stash the sheets of paper in the middle drawer of the rosewood desk in the study.

This is my final gambit. It is a goodbye embedded with a defiant hope. I don't know if it will stir anything in my son's declining memory, or in the childhood remembrances of my grandson, but I try to be optimistic. Sometimes all it takes is a madeleine, sometimes all it takes is a song like *The Lass of Aughrim*. And for any other reader, I hope it evokes an imaginative space. That is, perhaps one day you will be able to read this and know that there was more to Robert Ong Kok Peng than his undeserved writing accolades and his strained family ties.

In the end, it probably doesn't mean a thing that I've written this. Maybe no one will even see this thing I've struggled to create. Or maybe it will be mistaken for another one of Andrew's fantastical attempts at fiction, thereafter subject to misguided psychoanalyses and close readings. But it's all I can muster.

This is my last fiction, a last flailing attempt to live. If I can create, perhaps I can fight for my own existence. The fog closes in on me. I watch the embers of the dying light. Here is a last creation, a remembrance, perhaps, but also a plea. A plea for this moment, this life to last a little longer. A plea for something exceeding the past, a statement that I am not a remnant, that I am more than my projection. Every day that passes, I drift further away from the substance of sorrow. But this morning I touched Andrew's face while he was sleeping, or attempted to, as though he was a child again, and a grim discomfort surged through my arm. It felt cold, unnatural. I suppose it is a sign that I no longer belong here. And as I watched his face twitch, his addled brain becoming the last puzzle that he will grapple with, with memories falling out of place, all too momentarily, I felt it again. I knew sorrow once more. The fog is closing in. Waste away.

Mother

Mother, each day I look through your diaries and see this trail that you have left me. I read them to you as one reads a novel or a memoir, a chapter a day. In your dazed eyes I see no hint of recollection, but sometimes, there is a trace of acknowledgement.

When we get to the end, we'll probably start over again, one day at a time, until we reach that point in time again, when your memory failed, when your words left you, when you no longer knew my face. That's what life is, after all. The same old stories, repeated ad nauseum, meaning in the mundane, truth in the telling.

Now and then, you reach out to me, your hands trembling, cold. If you can no longer remember the days you've lived, the path you've taken through life, let me create for you anew this story from the fragments you have left me.

Void Deck

So imagine this: There are three people at the void deck. There is a middle-aged man, a chattier one, and a young woman seated around a stone table on stone stools. The meeting was not prearranged, and they do not know each other. This is, of course, a somewhat preposterous premise. In fact, as you go along, you will find incongruent details and unrealistic propositions. It doesn't matter. Just think of it all as a type of filling in the blanks. What's important is the story.

Until recently, these three people were new owners of flats in the block. Then each of them received some alarming news from a government agency with a name too long to commit to memory. To put it briefly, they lost their new homes to ghosts. The signs had always been there. They've all had supernatural encounters here before. The middle-aged man, for instance, once spotted a woman in an old Chinese costume outside his corridor window while advising his contractors about the details of the renovation work. With the windows shut, the talkative man has repeatedly encountered inexplicable gusts of wind and sharp changes in temperature in his home. The young woman first realized something was wrong when she heard voices along an empty corridor.

Typically, when a new HDB block is thought to be haunted, the policy is to leave it alone until the ghosts learn the sense to go away. (Of course, to qualify for this state of limbo, it is standard protocol for the block to have to meet the exacting standards of hauntedness first.) Sometimes, a little extra help is required from each of the major religions. Eventually, the block is declared safe for inhabitation after several years and meeting specific requirements.

On this occasion, however, there was an oversight. Paranormal activity was only confirmed after flat-balloting had taken place and people had moved in. This had no precedence in the history of Singapore housing development. Within two hours, the entire block was vacated. The lifts were deactivated. Eager tenants were evacuated, their moods considerably soured. Take what you need, leave what you can. Contractors abandoned their work mid-shift. Utilities inspectors ran for their lives. A sullen silence fell over the block like a blanket of dust.

Many of the new flat-owners found the news alarming. Some others cursed their luck. Most did not want anything to do with the ghosts because any association with the afterlife has been known to bring about bad luck. Not so the three here, however. They had to see it with their own eyes. But there was nothing to see, just an empty shell of an apartment block. And now they sit together, even though they have nothing in common except for this paranormal event. Very often, so little is sufficient to draw people together. They speak in hushed voices and their expressions betray wariness, even fear. They do not know how many ghosts inhabit the place, much less what exactly the ghosts are capable of. And yet, the fear of ghosts is not so much the fear of the unknown. Everybody knows that they are simply in the next stage of living, or at least, the next stage of existence. Nor is it quite the fear of the impossible. Most believe in the spirit, and by extension, must believe in the possibility of ghosts. And it is certainly not the fear of the unnatural, for there is nothing as natural as a ghost and as unnatural as civilization.

"I'm paying exorbitant sums for this flat," the middle-aged man says, "and now they're allocating me a different one three blocks away. I want to get what I paid for."

"Yes, me too," the talkative man chimes in. "It was such a good location, and now, my contractors have to redraw all their plans."

"And the fengshui too," the middle-aged man adds. "I paid thousands of dollars for the best fengshui master to plan my flat layout only to have them shift me somewhere else completely. A complete waste of money."

"I tried to see if there was any recourse, if we could be reimbursed for the deposits we've paid our contractors," the talkative man adds. "No such luck. I asked around for several hours until I uhh gave up the ghost."

He laughs, satisfied at his moment of cleverness. The middle-aged man does not catch the joke. The woman does not speak. She doesn't feel that she has anything to add.

"Nothing ever goes according to plan," the talkative man mutters even as he realizes that most things do.

"Did you see them?"

"Here, you mean?"

"Yes."

"No, but there were hot spots and cold spots."

"I saw one. It was unpleasant. What about you, girl?"

She shakes her head. "I just heard voices."

This is, of course, not the way a typical conversation in Singapore unfolds. No one here speaks like that. In vernacular, in word choice, in tone, in the artificially created back and forth rhythm of dialogue, none of this is realistic. But as I said, don't burden yourself with the details. Suspend your disbelief for a moment. The story's what's important.

The middle-aged man considers telling them about his own encounters with the supernatural. It is a risk because he barely knows them. He doesn't even know their names. They had merely met by coincidence, and what a coincidence. They had balloted for flats on the same floor and came back to it all at the same time. Still, new acquaintances are fickle things, and even the most miraculous coincidences are scant excuse for failing to play the social game properly. So he dithers, but eventually, quite unable to resist the temptation to share his own incredible tale, he speaks.

"I've seen one before," he begins. "I mean, before this. I've seen a ghost before. I was in the army, then. I had just enlisted, and I was doing my basic training. Back in those days, the army was so different. But I'll cut a long story short.

"The ghost was a little girl in a nice, expensive-looking dress. She always manifested in our bunk during the night, and usually, she would be sitting on top of one of our lockers.

"The first time I saw her, she was pointing at one of my bunkmates. She said, 'Sleeping.' Then she pointed at the next fellow. She said, 'Sleeping.' I was third, and when her finger turned towards me she said, 'Not sleeping.' Her face changed. She was angry. She jumped off the locker and marched towards my bed. Then she leant forwards and said into my ear, over and over again, 'Why are you not sleeping?'

"It was strange. I just couldn't move. And I don't know why I was so scared. She didn't hurt me, and maybe she couldn't hurt me. But I kept thinking that she would. I was terrified. I kept my eyes shut and mumbled a prayer.

"Eventually, I could feel my fingers again. Immediately, I got out of my bed. I ran outside and spent the night under a tree. Thankfully, no one saw me, so I didn't get punished by a sergeant. But every single night after that, I worried about seeing her again. And I did. Sometimes, I would hear her voice. Sleeping, sleeping, sleeping, and I would keep my eyes shut, hoping that she didn't notice I was still awake.

"I didn't tell anyone about it because I thought they would think I was crazy. I thought I was the only one who saw her until my buddy told me that he had seen a ghost one day. He described the whole thing to me, and I just kept nodding. I couldn't say a thing. He had seen her too. Everything he described, I recognized in my own experiences. The only difference was my friend didn't understand a word she said because he spoke only Hokkien. I think he found it even more frightening as a result. He didn't take it very well, but there was nothing we could do. No one else believed the story. It drove my friend crazy.

"One day, he told me that he was going for a check-up. I never saw him again. They all said that he had feigned insanity so that he could leave the army, but I knew that they were wrong.

"I asked around about the girl when I had finished my National Service. The story behind the girl is that she was adopted by a British family that had stayed around the area during the war. It's strange, though, come to think of it. After I left the army, everything seemed so different. Something had changed in me. Nothing was interesting anymore. I mean, don't get me wrong, my life hasn't been smooth-sailing, and I've seen some really strange things in my life, but nothing quite as interesting as the little girl on the locker. I just feel a bit, he hesitates, empty."

He looks up at his two new acquaintances and wonders if their expressions are conveying stupefaction or mockery.

"There are so many ghost stories in the army," the talkative man says. "I remember one about a mother who committed suicide and haunted the obstacle course where her son had died in an accident. There was also one about a soldier being haunted by his buddy. They just can't leave us alone. Upon saying that, he laughed, until stern expressions told him that he was the only one who found it funny."

"Do you have any theories about ghosts?" the middle-aged man asks.

"Theories?"

"Like how they exist, where they exist, and why they exist?"

"I think they have things left to do. Love, revenge, broken promises. That's what all the movies say."

"Things they can't let go of."

"I think they're trapped," the middle-aged man says. "They've left our world and can't get to the next, stuck in the space in between."

"Like some kind of purgatory," the woman says.

He cocks his head and turns his ear toward her. "What?"

"Purgatory," she repeats.

He moves his ear closer.

"Never mind," she says. "Never mind."

"I first saw him in the mirror." This sudden outburst by the talkative man leaves the others taken aback. "My son, I mean."

Their faces express their concern and astonishment. He pays them no heed.

"I probably shouldn't be telling you about this, but . . . " He pauses. The silence is grim. "He was five years old. He fell from the window. We lived on the seventeenth floor."

"Was it three or four years ago?" the woman interrupts. "I think I remember. It was in the papers."

"Yes, four years ago. About a week after he died, we began to hear voices. His toys began moving on their own. And one evening we saw him. It was just his back that we saw as he ran and turned at a corner. We thought we were imagining things. And then it happened with increasing frequency. He was in his old room a lot of the time. Sometimes he would come to ours in the middle of the night. My wife would scream now and then while she was showering because she saw him in the mirror. She was a real mess then. We all were."

And in his mind now, he recalls not her expressions exactly, but a shivering, skittering caricature of a woman. He remembers her words inaccurately, words true to the spirit of the moment and yet never spoken, words that perhaps ring even truer. Most of all, he remembers shades of her expressions, like brush strokes on canvas, always precisely and yet never definitely.

"We just wanted to get on with our lives. So we moved. I thought everything would be okay once we found a new place, but I was wrong. The boy followed us. We moved again, and then again. We moved a total of four times, sometimes buying, sometimes renting. This is our fifth address."

These may seem drastic actions to take, especially to avoid a consciousness that is in essence one's son, but sometimes the fear of ghosts exceeds the ideas of kith and kin.

"We jumped through so many hoops over the years and dealt with obstacle after obstacle. We met all kinds of people and completed all sorts of procedures. Honest property agents, dishonest property agents, application forms, reapplication forms, balloting and re-balloting. We got so used to it. The point is, we've been running for a very long time. At first, it felt like I had something to fear, but then I got used to the running, and after that, it was just going through the motions. We were just drifting."

"Did you try to get help?"

"Psychiatrists were useless. She wasn't crazy. I had seen him too. I was just better at pretending that I hadn't. We also thought of seeking help from religious groups. We were afraid that they would turn us away because we've never been particularly religious. We believed in a bit of everything but never everything of something. It also didn't seem too kind to perform exorcisms on our own son. He never seemed particularly vengeful or tormented. We just— We just couldn't deal with the idea of it all. It's all just too much.

"It had other effects on our lives too. We've never stayed in anything higher than the third floor, and we've not had children since.

"But here's the funny thing. One day, I woke up in the middle of the night. It was quiet. I could hear the air-con and the sound of my wife's breathing. It was so quiet, the quietness was terrifying. It was like the whole world had gone away. I sat there thinking about my son and I realized that I didn't know why I had been running. Do something for long enough and the reasons will lose their meaning.

"It didn't stop me from running. Like I said, this is number five."

He pauses, before asking: "What traps a ghost in its existence?" His two new acquaintances just shrug. The only things we know for sure about ghosts come from our ghost stories.

"Do you think they live forever?" he asks, unaware of the absurdity of his question.

"Forever is a very long time," she remarks.

"Too much time," he says. "Forever is too much time."

He stops here. He wants to go on but doesn't find the words to do so. The man's grin vanishes. The inflections of his voice shift. There is a change in his demeanour like the fall of dusk. And for an instant, he believes that he sees his son from the corner of his eye. He hears the trace of his voice, spots the echo of his shadow. He can hardly bear to look. The child's nervous shape, his fractured voice, his faded shadow. It is his son. It is not his son.

He does not say a word to these two acquaintances of his, but they notice the changes that have overcome him, his face now tangled up in distress, his expression revealing an emotion not called guilt, grief, or gloom. These terms are too laden with the political, psychoanalytical, and philosophical. For our purpose, let us simply call it an expression of suffering. And then he holds his hands to his face, and even if for an instant, he becomes a shivering, skittering caricature of a man. And then he begins to weep.

"I'm sorry," he says upon regaining some composure.

"Don't be," she tells him.

A long and calm silence. No one speaks, as if there is nothing more to be said. We all have too much to be sorry for, and no one to forgive us. The universe goes still for these three gathered, once neighbours-to-be, and now trading ghost stories like students around a campfire.

"What about you?" the middle-aged man asks the woman suddenly.

"Me?"

"Have you seen ghosts before?"

She hesitates.

"It's okay if you don't want to share."

"I think I have," she is quick to say.

A pause.

"It was my boyfriend. He died in a car accident. I loved him very much."

"I'm sure you did."

"We had been together for two years. We met during an economics class in the university. A small truck ran into him in Melbourne while he was on an exchange programme. I wasn't there to see him die."

"I'm sorry to hear that."

"It's okay. I've moved on, I think. I'm married now. My husband's coming to pick me up later."

She pauses as if looking for the strength that will allow her to continue telling her story.

"I saw him once. My dead boyfriend, I mean. I was sitting in my bed because the night was so humid, and I couldn't get to sleep. I looked out of my window, and I saw a figure across the street. I stay on the third floor, so I could see it quite clearly. There wasn't a single car on the road. The orange streetlights lit the bare concrete and gravel up like it was a stage. He was standing there in a smart shirt and jeans. He was clearly looking in the direction of my window, but he didn't seem to be able to see me. I waved my arms at him, trying to get his attention, but he didn't respond. I called out to him, so loudly that I'm sure the neighbours must have heard me, but he must have been too far away. I wanted to go to him, but I couldn't. It felt like I was not allowed. So I just watched. I just kept watching him until I fell asleep.

"I didn't see him again after that, but I could never shake the feeling that he was always right next to me. Sometimes, I would hear his voice or feel his breath on the nape of my neck, and then I'd turn around and he would be gone. It was almost as if he was afraid to see me.

"I couldn't bear it. I didn't understand why he had to die, and why I couldn't see him again. I didn't understand a thing."

She doesn't falter. This surprises her. She expected her voice to fall to pieces, was sure that there would be tears in her eyes. And yet, she is, by any measure, perfectly calm.

"One day, I told my parents about it and they looked very concerned. I told my friends and they all said I was crazy, that I had been depressed and I'd been imagining things, so I didn't say anything about it anymore. They all looked at me like I was losing it. I can still remember their expressions. I hated those expressions. It was like I couldn't say what I meant, like this thing that happened to me didn't fit into anyone else's experience of society.

"Anyway, the encounters stopped after a while. Maybe he had to go. Maybe he gave up. Or maybe I had imagined it all. I figured that maybe my friends had a point. I must have imagined his ghost, and it was time that I grew up, moved on. I can't help thinking that they were right all along, which frightens me because it means I've gotten over him. I've left him behind. And now I can't even remember his face."

Those last words fall as the petals of a withering rose fall. A tired analogy, perhaps, yet one that is nevertheless true. A frown appears across her face.

"Don't you have photos?"

"It's not the same. That's not him."

It's true. Photographs are sketches that conjure nothing of a person. Photographs are demonstrations of death, embodying completeness, irretrievability, impressions, memories, interpretations.

"It's strange. Everything else becomes so hollow and so robotic. Nothing had really changed, yet everything seemed so different. School, work, family, friends—it was dull, meaningless, and unbearable. Maybe I have a new perspective of the world around me. I don't know. I just want to see him again."

She fiddles with her bracelet. It helps her to keep her nerve. If only she could see him beside her now. There he is, his profile fuzzy and his features vague, as if standing behind a fog.

She does not notice him. Perhaps she cannot notice him. Or perhaps she has over time convinced herself that these visitations are merely figments of her imagination. No matter. Instead, watch as he caresses her cheek, speaks her name, and watches her stillness. And then, only dismay.

He doesn't know for how much longer he will love her. He does not know if he loves her still. It is only a matter of time. He is nothing but a matter of time. Long after he has forgotten love, he will still be repeating patterns without their meanings, like most ghosts who repeat the same routines long after time has robbed them of their significance. There is a moment when all the things in the brittle frames of our lives pass into the illusion of remembrance, and for the departed, it is the moment that they truly die.

There are three people at the void deck. The meeting was not prearranged. Around them, unnoticed and invisible, silhouettes and shapes congregate, some shimmering and others dull. Through walls and pillars, they emerge, passing through concrete as drifters pass through life. Slowly, the ghosts gather, chained to little more than memories false, fragile, and fickle. Listen to the murmurs. Perhaps it is that they too tell stories, their last defence against the tyranny of being. One can never be sure, but after all, what else avails them?

At the void deck, a curious congregation occurs. Human and ghost, often side by side, occasionally even overlapping, yet always distant, speaking to one another without hearing each other, different but the same. Storytellers telling stories, stories being told. Dead things desperately seeking what is alive.

The chatter of the evening birds falls upon their ears. The block stands lifeless—one of many in this crowded city—a faceless stele under a sun drained of its blood, and a sky of a foreign colour. And far away, an unreachable horizon. Time passes. Time always passes. Among the absent connections, in this empty space, they gather—the always departing and the forever departed—with nothing but stories, nothing but words, and when even the words desert us, nothing but silence; not quite living, and not quite dead.

The Way of the Flesh

First, I wait for the darkness. It is necessary that the process take place under dim conditions, for the spirit cannot bear the caustic light. The dead are not creatures of the morning. The dead seek the earth and the detritus.

It has been four months and thirteen days since she left. To be honest, I had not expected it to take so long. I thought things would be settled within a week. She did not return on the seventh day, as would be Chinese tradition. Perhaps I hadn't been pious enough. Perhaps I had neglected to set things up correctly, made some mistake, a misstep in the complicated tangle of this cosmic machinery. No matter.

I keep track of things in a small diary. I no longer trust the experience of time. Ever since her death, the days bleed into one another. It still feels like last week even if it has been months. Time has become an elastic notion. The diary has become the way I measure time. Tonight, I write one last entry in the diary. I am sure of it. Tonight is the thirtieth experiment.

That's what I've preferred to call them, but they really are just rituals. Some involve incantations, some involve blood, and some involve animal sacrifice. All of them draw from the power of belief. All rituals are a matter of conviction.

None of them have worked yet, but I have a good feeling about tonight. I think this is when it will all fall into place. This is when I will see her again. We're running out of time, after all, whether that means we will finally succeed or if her spirit loses its grip on our material realm and we are confined to eternal separation. I'm not an expert on these matters but it stands to reason. I could just take my own life, but who is to say that we will end up in the same place? And who is to say that we will remember each other? I'd much rather bring her back.

The process is elaborate. I have spent a whole week preparing for it. In essence, I need to lead Grace's spirit back to our material plane. To do that, I must descend to an intermediate state of being. I must be able to perceive her, and she me. And from there, we will walk together, either on this new road of ours or further into hell.

She lies on our bed, rotted and still. The worms have finally arrived. Immediately after her death, I went out of the house and put plans into motion. I did everything I could within the limits of my skills to preserve her body. You can find most of this information online. Putting it into practice is a different story. I did my best, taking as much care as I could. An embalmed body nevertheless decays a week or so after the process, but it takes longer, much longer, for the worms to set in. Forgive me, Grace. I didn't want to subject you to this unnatural process of preservation, to fix the state of your body into some false permanence, dragging your body further away from its materiality. A body without life is just a thing. But I had to. I needed time. I seek the return of your ghost. And tonight might be the night.

What does a ghost look like? Don't ask me. I was always one of the sceptics. It seemed impossible to believe that there was anything left after the raucous chaos of life. It made no sense to me. We never think that a candle's flame survives its extinguishing. We never ask a moth of its afterlife. Indeed, we are rarely, if ever, haunted by the ghosts of frogs or roaches or extinct animals. The only true ghosts are semiotic in nature. The things that take on a life after a life simply because people remember them, mutate them, refuse to let go. Besides, the physics of hauntings make no sense. Everything we know about thermodynamics and biology suggests that at the end there is just cold nothingness. The fate of everything is that it dissipates. It decays into nothingness, or at least, is transformed into something else. Things merely leave one form to take another. But we are not energy, after all. Like the stars, we are swirling masses of chaos. Like the stars, we all burn out.

We met at work, flung together by the whims of fate. We fell rapidly in love despite being utter strangers to begin with. In love, everything is coincidence masquerading as destiny. Things developed quickly. She was young, and so I was surprised she agreed to marry me. Perfect story, really. You should never expect anything to work out. Nothing ever goes according to plan, until they do. There were eleven years between us. And on the day that we got married, I felt the tremendous burden of time. All relationships begin on the premise that one will leave before the other, and with our age difference, I was certain that she had drawn the short end of the stick. Surely, she would outlive me by a number of years and would have to live with the burden of grief, for love is a curse that outlives living, woven into the fabric of memory and the nervous system. Love and desire do not exist without the body. We are nothing but desiring systems, libido machina.

Who knew, of course, that she would be so tormented by illness at the end of her life. Who knew that she would be first to depart.

Focus. I need to focus now.

Her hair has become greasy and matted, the strands withered, their ends frayed. Parts of her skin now have a papery texture. Parts of it have turned a deep maroon. Some of her muscles have become desiccated, whereas other have become soft and clammy. The decay is eating into her flesh, and out of her body as well. To witness this decomposition always leaves me in a state of wonder, a reminder of our constant state of becoming. One moment to the next, one metamorphosis after another. I take in the putrid scent of the rot. Perhaps we seek little more in life than a final destiny, the end of the sentence from which our meaning can be determined. That is the appeal of eternity, the point of the afterlife, the trust in some kind of forever. But no, I refuse this. We exist in the flow of time. We don't seek pronouncements but transformations, continuations, decompositions.

I think of the tale of Izanagi, the creator deity of Japanese myth, who ventures into the land of the dead in search of his sister-wife Izanami. Breaking a promise not to look, he finds that she is a decaying corpse. In shame, she declares vengeance, vowing to kill a thousand people a day, only for Izanagi to counter that he would create a thousand and five hundred. It is a tale mired in death. Unable to handle the state of her decay, they both choose rejection. Like some kind of anti-Orpheus, they decided against love. But with its focus on the split, the tale occludes the nature of human love, its persistence, how it clings to life and memory like a lingering sigh. Love dogs us like a curse.

Lighting the candles is the seventh step. As the faint, flickering lights illuminate the room, I take note of the shadows dancing across the walls. The blurred flutters of darkness. The outline of a tree dragged into a long diagonal shape. It is a windy night. There might be a storm coming.

Initially, there was grief, no, something more visceral, more primal, something beyond words. Grief is processed, narrativized. Grief is recognized trauma. What I experienced was more feral, more blind, like a clarion call from my reptilian brain. That is, after her death, despite my best efforts, I found myself wracked with pain. Merely existing was agonizing. Although I had already charted out the days ahead with my plans to reunite us, although I had spent weeks imagining the worst, I was still defeated by my own emotions, my own tears, my own biochemistry. But there is no shame in that. Grief is the whole point of this. Every romance begins at the end, when we confront the fact of its transience. Some of us put it aside for as long as we can. Some of us prepare for the end the moment we begin. I had that decision made for me. From the moment she fell ill, we knew that we had to make the most out of the time we had left. We spent all the energy and time we could spare planning. As she arranged how she wanted to die, I was formulating a plan to ensure that it would not be our last goodbye. I became obsessive. I don't mind admitting it. This ambition became my whole life.

I wonder if she would have done the same for me. But in truth there's no point wondering. If this succeeds, I might be able to ask her. To be honest, I have no idea if any of these rituals would work out, but I portioned my savings out across the most promising options and hoped for the best. I worked out a plan to try out as many of them as possible, with sufficient rest and preparation time in between. I didn't want to tire myself out before I had exhausted all these options. I purchased the necessary materials and paid for expert advice, and beyond that, I reduced all my expenditure to just basic sustenance. In fact, I have been eating less and less, which is just as well, because there were some unforeseen costs. I sold everything I could think of and emptied my bank account. These things are costly, but material possessions are merely a passage to immaterial means.

If most religions are to be believed, then there is very little point to this. Particularly in belief systems where the soul is eternal. Our eventual reunion would be eternal. To be frank, eternity is a disgusting concept. That which cannot die is an aberration. And yet, despite my clarity on the issue, the prospect still appeals. I don't know what to do with these contradictory beliefs. I mean, what are we supposed to do in the meantime? Just suffer through the days? Just accept things, let go, move on? I understand why people peddle this rhetoric, but I knew early on that that was not the path I wanted to take. Why do we have to accept our grief?

Move on, catch up with us, with the rest of the cruel universe, bear with the pain with a stone-cold heart. Yes, they always say that you should move on, but the term seems so poorly described that it is more aggravating than useful. There is no practical advice, there is no comfort to be drawn from it. Worse, it even comes across as dismissive and meaningless. I get it. I know that I must somehow live with the imperative of fitting into the society around me. But in the realm of words and logics and meanings, instead of the ineffable sphere of raw feeling, I know I am but a cog in the functioning of this distorted society, constructed from these processions and processes. Do we really deal with our grief, or do we simply shelve it somewhere, sight unseen?

True grief is a bodily response, a material manifestation of the crushing sadness that results from our confrontation with the failure of our belief systems. I too once bought into the convincing lie of being at peace with death. But when confronted with the brutal finality of no possible return, how swiftly your beliefs can change. I had to do something about this pain, to give it shape, to render it into new meaning and protect it from the logics of the world, this pain which is mine.

Her body lies still on the bed as it usually has in these past weeks, only ever moved when required for any experiments. With the increased fragility of the tissue, it has become more and more dangerous to move her body around. Of course, I never reported her death. After all, I would probably need the body. This was uncharted territory, at least for most of mainstream science. I took no chances. Besides, how long could a spirit be tethered to this material world without its vessel to anchor it? I held onto the body for as long as I could, this mortal shell, this flesh-thing.

On top of that, I absolutely did not want the authorities to have anything to do with her. They would just take her away and initiate all the processes and procedures, turning her death into a legality, trapped in legalese and bureaucracy, devoid of true meaning. Wakes, funerals, cremations and burials. Rituals of a different sort. The saddest sort of afterlife, rote and prescribed, unable to mean anything. Why would I subject the love of my life to that mundane procession? Funerary services and caskets are already a massive industry, and on top of that, it is filled with scammers and charlatans. And I too would become a part of this industry of lies, performing my pain in front of her friends like Hamlet performing his undying love by leaping in and desecrating his lover's grave, staging the most ironic performance of his already very ironic life.

Her death became my secret. It was easy. We never interacted with many people, and her sister only calls once a month at the most. I simply texted her and told her that we would be travelling for a couple of months. Then I made more excuses. A short-term fix, but that was all I needed. I merely stalled for time. Lately her sister has been getting concerned, but we're at the end of this journey anyway. It doesn't matter anymore.

I touch the hollow of Grace's cheek. I think of the days when I could still hear her voice. Why am I even doing this? Why am I so attached to that which is nothing but a shell? It's only natural. This is me refusing to let go. This is me seeking possibilities new.

I need to get a move on. With a knife, I draw a bit of blood from the palm of my right hand. The blood trickles down my fingers, viscous, as I draw a circle around the bed. The pain startles me at first, but I think back to Grace's last days, her body poisoned with such agony. She no longer was the person that I had once known. Her every utterance was a cry for help. Her face had turned gaunt, ghoulish. Her eyes seemed to sink into her skull. And her entire frame was pallid and emaciated.

Grace, we will be together again soon.

The circle must not be broken. Master Pu was very clear about this. I don't know what would happen if it were to be broken. Perhaps her spirit would be unable to hold its shape. Perhaps some supernatural force would be let loose upon the world. Whatever it is, I will not allow such desecration. This circle will concentrate the energies in this space. All existences are distillations of some cosmic imagination, after all, threads of fiction tangled in a particular moment in time, a particular point in space. A wind seems to stir from within the confines of this enclosed room, defying the logics of the world.

I found Master Pu through a series of introductions, a friend of a friend talking to a friend of a friend, that sort of thing. After weeks of arrangements, we finally met in a quiet park in the dead of night. She was a small woman, so wizened that her face was covered in creases and her hands resembled the knots of a tree. She wielded silence to great effect and would only speak when absolutely necessary. Her instructions were written on a piece of paper that her assistant handed to me. She asked for no payment, only that I heed her warnings. This, she said, was a ritual with enormous risks, and suggested that there was a possibility I could lose my life. She also warned sternly that I was not to deviate from her instructions in the slightest. What was in it for her? I'm not sure. She spoke briefly about her belief that the body is the vessel through which the universe expresses itself. Every twitch, every ache, every sigh is but a thread in its fabric. There is a purer form, she said, in which we may exist. That is the form that we are after. It confused me then, but I am slowly coming round to it. No matter. We are here on the cusp of reunion anyway.

I write one last diary entry. My handwriting's going awry. I try to keep it as reportage, but the memories don't stop. It's all coming back, like the lashings of a whip or the torrents of a river.

we were young

There are no events, no narratives, nothing to occlude you. It is just you as you were. I remember. I remember the feel of your hand. I always loved the feel of your hand and the sensation of our fingers interlocking. I remember your charisma. I also remember the curve of your shoulders and the circumference of your arms. Your feet, your toes. I remember your eyes as you look at me. You open your mouth to speak. There is a measure of uncertainty here. I am not sure if I remember your voice. I can't

old in these remembrances

older than I've ever been

I don't even recognize my hands.

Incomprehension—it eats away at my feeble mind. I relent. I surrender.

There is a mirror in the room. I have not dared to look at it much lately. Perhaps I fear becoming too attached to my existing shape. I know that I have changed. I stagger to my feet again and drag this tired shape to the mirror. The sight that greets me is gaunt and warped. Unsurprising, since grief is twisted flesh, contorted into the agony of being, the pain of the heart expanding beyond its limits, bloated, distorted. I must embrace this. I mustn't deny the way of the flesh. That's what Master Pu said. In our embrace of the eternal soul, do we too become hollowed like the stories we tell ourselves? Are we fated to be nothing more than myth? It is the chaos that we must surrender to.

I once read a variant of the Christian creation myth, in which Adam stumbles upon the creation of the first woman mid-process and is so disgusted that he has to turn away. The interrupted project was so disturbing to the man that God restarted the process from scratch. Perhaps Adam was made to forget. I don't remember how the story goes. I don't even remember the book where I found it. I only recall that there was a reset. I pity Adam, ironically unable to love his one companion because of how he had seen the biological machinery inside us.

What love are we capable of if we are repulsed by their basic biology? How could we be so enamoured by ourselves yet so disgusted by our own creation that we would need this sheath concealing our inner workings? Superficial creatures in every sense of the word.

A few nights ago, I had a vision of Grace, glowing in her decay. I could see all the signs of life pulsating underneath her skin, the peristaltic movements, the rhythmic contractions of the heart and lungs, all internal workings showing through a glorious translucency. Master Pu was right, that deep at the heart of our universe is a churning chaos. We are children of the cosmos.

I must seek what lies underneath our façades. At the possible cost of my life, I will approach your reality. I have no regrets. I made up my mind early on that I would commit to this course of action. This is but a small price to pay. I look at your rotting shadow, look at the tangle of creatures feasting on your flesh, a roiling mass that almost seems to speak to me, as if attempting to relay to me the true meaning of existence. The stench speaks to our potential to return to our basic existence, free from language, free from politics, free from the struggles of this bodily apparatus, only the logic of the universe, reunited in the freest expression of our existence.

Just say something. It's been so long since I heard your voice. You can't even begin to imagine that that feels like. So here we are—a man with all the wrong words and a woman with none. The silence is terrible. It's the only thing that means what it says. All the noises of the world cannot possibly hope to usurp it. And that's why you have to speak again.

I wonder if you can you hear me. Grace?

You're skinny, stretched, skewed. Why do you look so sallow? You're a shadow, a pale shadow, and me, I'm not even that.

You can no longer answer me.

The memories speak

to me

see how old I am, and how old you are. I reminiscence, I think of times when you were young. Is it nostalgic? Is it romantic? Is it purely sexual? I can't be sure. I know, however, that people always change. How does one expect constancy and devotion in love? We are both different persons from one instant to the next. How do we find love in the fickleness of human nature, the withering curse of biology, and the

the

Time passes. What happens to us?

We are at the end. Now I simply have to imbibe this cloudy concoction. This is a poison. I swirl the murky liquid and draw the glass closer to my lips. I almost vomit at the smell. A hacking cough. I fail to quell my body's resistance as it summons convulsions. But no, I must hold it in. As the liquid flows into my mouth, I am surprised by how smoothly it all goes. It tastes foul, but my throat does not seize. My body doesn't reject it. I'm so close to seeing her again. I think back to how things have come to this. I think back to my obsession. I had grown so fixated on the idea that something like that has become reasonable to me now. Tenderness intermingling with unbearable pain. This may kill me, but the yearning has become too strong. I must draw myself closer to death in order to bridge the divide, between Grace and I, between the rational mind and the chaotic cosmos. I am Izanagi, ready to rescue his bride. I am Orpheus, ready to redeem his love.

I prepare the bed. Something's not right. It doesn't feel right. I might not have much time left. Was it always supposed to be this way? I sprinkle dried hyacinths across the blanket. The sheets have turned to a shade between ochre and the colour of pus. The smell of the flowers is both vegetal and sickly sweet. I take my place beside her. And now we wait.

The darkness is creeping. It has taken on a life of its own. I no longer trust my flesh-eyes. That is part of the process, to abandon these conditioned physical senses, the chains of biochemistry, and surrender to the disorder of this bodily blight. I think of your voice again. I see your face in the encroaching darkness. Seconds trickling into minutes, their flow ever slowing.

The wind rises. I turn to you and embrace your frame. I look into the sunken hollows of your eyes, where once burned the embers of life, now only abyss. I feel the crawling of the decomposition on my ragged skin. May this intimate foulness unravel me. I embrace it. I embrace it the way I embrace you. The worms crawl over my limbs and indulge in voracious mastication. Let them feast. Their ravenous appetite spreads like a psoriasis across my skin, puncturing this wretched sheath, tearing into muscle, into sinew, through the fibre of my being, seeking bone and bile. Take me into the dirt with you. My beloved grotesque. I succumb to the worm.

What if this fails? Have I made the wrong decision? Will this poison kill me? I feel the flesh tearing itself off the bone. I feel my skin peeling off my person. Briefly I think about what will be found in the days after, two grotesque shapes crumbling in their wretched forms. Like in that old tale. A vision, two bodies lying together, half-eaten by the universe.

Something stirs in the congealed darkness. A movement so slight as to be nearly imperceptible. Is that starlight on the ceiling? The glint of the cosmos? Flickering, multiplying. A breath. The warmth of a breath falls on the side of my neck. I wonder if I've imagined it, but no, I need to trust my senses, I need to believe. No, these are not hallucinations. I can feel the rising and falling of your chest. I can feel the gentle twitch of your arm. My love, is that you?

And then, a guttural noise. The tortured stretching of the vocal cords. The wheezing of punctured lungs. Are you trying to speak, my love? It's me. I'm here. I can feel you coming back to life, birthed anew. Do you see me? We must meet on the same plane before I can bring you back. A shriek engulfing me in your presence again. Your voice is nothing but a screech, reduced to its primal quality. Can you see me? You howl so viciously, so recklessly, that I can only assume you are still blind. Your body writhes in the agony of a fractured existence. I need to take this further. I need you to see me so that I can lead you back. Take me with you, drag me through the earth in the throes of the same wracking pain that you were subjected to. I will hold you tighter, sinking into the earth, into the detritus, so that my person is unmasked by the tender agony of decay. All things are façade. I seek that which crawls, that which squirms, that which moulders and putrefies.

I feel my own decay. I see myself gangrenous, festering, destroyed. Here my journey begins. I will wade into this river until I meet you again. I will embrace the suffering of love and grief. The body is nothing but pain, and it is this pain that verifies the core of our existence. I will walk the same path you have walked to meet you on the same moment, in the same place. I embrace you in your filth, freed of language and logic and thought. Hello,

Grace.

Ghost

One morning, a ghost appeared in the corner of the room. It was damp and green, like a mossy sponge. The ghost was a mound about four feet tall, and on its uneven surface, there were relief configurations that almost looked like a face. I wasn't afraid, even though it was like nothing I had ever seen before, and it had no reason to be there. In fact, there was a certain calmness about its presence, as though it had always belonged in the room, in that corner, as though it was finally ready to make its presence known to me.

I wasn't sure what to do about it. To be frank, I had spent my entire life being sceptical of the paranormal—specifically when it came to the existence of ghosts. But I had also spent my entire life being a coward. Horror movies were always able to make me jump even if I didn't believe in ghosts.

At first, this unexpected turn of events left me unsure of what to do. I wasn't even certain that I could believe my eyes. Reality takes time to settle down—to properly percolate— immediately after one wakes up. So I waited for five minutes and looked again—but the ghost remained. I stayed in the bed for a long time, not because I was afraid, but because nothing in my admittedly shallow life experience could tell me what to do. I stayed still and observed for what must have been a quarter of an hour. It was certainly alive though it made almost no sound.

Eventually, I climbed out of bed and approached it gingerly, for fear of frightening it. It was only when I drew nearer that I could see the crags and pores across its surface. It didn't seem to be breathing, but can the human eye really observe a sponge or a starfish breathing?

I thought of calling up my friend to let her know that there was a ghost in the room. It was her place, after all, and as temporary caretaker, it was my responsibility to let her know about such unexpected developments. But I hesitated. There was a harmlessness—no, helplessness—to the ghost that gave pause. I didn't want to snitch on the ghost. I didn't want to be the bad guy. Maybe it would be gone the next day.

My friend had asked me to look after her place for six months while she was away. She was an academic from Sichuan who had to take on a project back home, but there was no way she could suspend her rental agreement. It was just more efficient for her to put someone else in the guest room to take care of the miscellaneous chores, and not let the rent go to waste. As a writer working freelance jobs just to put Gardenia bread on the table, I accepted the offer to have a place to myself for six months, so that I could complete a novel about a conman falling out of pace with modern times that had been derailed by my freelance work. That is, I thought of it as kind of a friendship writing residency. The guestroom featured a desk, power sockets galore, a simple bed, Wi-Fi, and some decorations. I was also allowed to use the kitchen so long as I kept it clean. My duties included watering the plants, checking the mail, collecting parcels, and the occasional light cleaning. And of course, I was to take care of any water and electricity bills that came.

We first met as university classmates several years ago, when I still aspired to become a scientist. She said that she had taken up a government scholarship and had come from Zigong. At the time, I knew nothing about Zigong, and the only thing that she told me was that many dinosaurs came from Zigong. I had always had a fondness for dinosaurs, and I guess that's why, even though we had almost nothing in common, we became fast friends. When she mentioned it, I started rambling on and on about fossils and why they were so fascinating to me. I haven't mentioned this yet, but I'm kind of socially inept.

Fossils had always fascinated me because they felt like objects from a different reality, things that had time travelled. The joint was out of its time, so to speak. Emerging again millions of years after their initial formation, they had all effectively shed their immediate substance to become symbols, texts, to be interpreted in a language invented millions of years after the instance of death. That is, despite their very material existence—bones, amber, petrified wood, oil, DNA—there was nothing left of the body, no breathing, circulation, digestion. Just texts, words, signs. Like semiotic ghosts of a sort.

I decided to call my grandmother instead. She was sure to have an answer. She was the only family I had, and we lived in a small flat in Toa Payoh. In order to ensure that I made the most of this time I set aside for myself, I tried not to go home too much. I wanted to adhere to a strict regimen over this time to ensure that I would concentrate on my writing. I wanted it to feel different from my usual routine. Grandma was fairly independent despite her age, which helped me to take up this temporary isolation scheme.

Grandma spoke primarily Cantonese, but she always spoke to me in Mandarin because, when I was growing up she believed that it would help me in school. An approximate translation of our exchange:

"Grandma, I saw a—"

"Have you eaten?"

"I'm fine. I saw— I mean, how about you?"

"I've just had lunch."

"That's great. Uh, Grandma, I uh—"

"Yes?"

"I think I saw a ghost, Grandma."

"What?"

"Yeah, it's short, and dirty green, and kind of—"

"A ghost?"

"Kind of damp. It doesn't really have a face but— I just know it's a ghost."

She didn't say a word.

"It just appeared in the corner of the room. It's still sitting there."

There was a long, long silence. It was at about that point that I realized I was never really going to get through to her. Certainly, people of her generation were likely to have a greater appreciation of the spiritual or indeed the paranormal, but my grandmother was also a devout Christian, so she was never really into the whole ghosts and ghouls thing. I don't really think anyone can deduce all that much from a silence across a phone line, but it didn't seem like she was mad or panicking. She was probably just trying to figure out a reasonable explanation for my behaviour.

"Never mind," I said. "It'll probably be gone tomorrow."

She didn't refer to it again for the rest of the phone call, and I chipped in too, doing my best to pretend that everything was okay, and that I hadn't really called her to talk about Casper the Friendly Ghost. We talked for another 15 minutes, and through it all, I didn't look away from the ghost. It was almost imperceptible, but there was a change in its demeanour, as though it was comforted by the sound of a human voice.

It wasn't gone the next day, so I accepted the fact that I was staying in a haunted house.

You might wonder how I knew it was a ghost at first sight. After all, it could have been any manner of strange creature. Was it glowing? Did it send me visions of its former life? Were there tell-tale signs of ectoplasm? I can only say that, no, there was no objective indicator that it was a ghost, but there are some things that you just *know*. Also, my friend had told me that someone had died in her flat once.

That afternoon, I decided that I would take care of the ghost—which isn't to say that I was going to have it exterminated—but that I would look after its needs. I felt a kind of obligation. On a logical level, I never quite understood the fear of ghosts that people often claimed to have anyway. Certainly, much of it comes out of a fear of the unknown that characterizes the afterlife, but most ghost stories also preferred malicious renditions, which always disturbed me. After all, weren't human ghosts once human beings too? It seemed unfair to assume that they were all malevolent by default.

For the first five days, the ghost didn't do anything. Every so often, it appeared to drift a little to the left or right, but this appeared to be its natural pulse, and its average position never changed as far as I could tell.

It didn't need to eat (I checked). Or drink (I checked too).

The ghost had a voice. Sometimes, it would be a whimper like the slow release of air from a balloon. Sometimes it would be a wheeze, not unlike a leaky whistle. And sometimes, it would be a humming, not like a refrigerator or a computer, but like a very old person who didn't realise that they were doing it. Most of the time, however, it was silent, and even at its loudest, it was never enough to cause me any disturbance.

On the sixth day, it showed off a new trick. Every so often, the ghost—as if it really was the sponge that it resembled—would release a colourless, odourless liquid onto the vinyl floor. This happened irregularly and silently, but I liked to think that the ghost was embarrassed about it, so I mopped up the fluid on the ground each time. I'm sure I must have imagined it but each time I glanced at the terrestrial feature that I supposed was its face, there seemed to be a look of appreciation.

Other than that, nothing else of significance happened. This continued for weeks. I got used to its presence, and perhaps it got used to mine. No, it wasn't just a matter of presence, but the individual rhythms of our existence, the things we did in a day, our moods, our tempers. It crossed my mind again to report this incident to my friend, but by then the ghost and I were so well-acquainted that it felt like a betrayal. Besides, my friend had said that it was suicide, that some twenty years ago someone took their own life in this house. That only made me even more sympathetic.

I went out and took a few books out from the public library, all of which were ghost stories of some sort. I thought that they might help me understand my situation somehow, and in turn, help my writing. Sure, that makes almost no sense, but then again, neither did my situation.

There was some *Mad Max* weather outside, so I came home quickly and spent my afternoon reading. I especially enjoyed the books collecting Japanese kaidan as the spirits in them clearly represented living aspects of the world, while their ghosts tended to have believable, sympathetic motives.

Surveying the different portrayals of our ethereal friends, I came to realize that the concept of ghosts always elicited sympathy for me. You see, ghosts are stuck in time. They are a way that memories manifest. They cannot leave their moment. They don't perform the daily rituals that mark the passing of our days—eating, shitting, sleeping. They don't change their clothes. They don't age. Most ghosts haunt not a place, but a moment—or more accurately, a memory, a story, a trauma. They cannot abandon this station; hence they cannot create anything new. There is nothing left for them, nothing ahead except deep unrest.

So, being empty, ghosts are little more than photographs or scars, stories that tell themselves, essentially memories. In that, I suppose we all become ghosts, sooner or later.

I called Grandma again. Initially, I was ready to pester her about this ghost again, thinking that my insistence would eventually win her over. However, this determination dissolved the moment I heard her voice, which was tired, gentle, and familiar. She didn't say much except to ask, *Are you sure you're taking care of yourself?* I thought of the number of times I had lied to her when she'd ask the same question before. I didn't say a thing, but she must have heard me sigh. Suddenly, this whole writing business seemed ridiculous, as though I had abandoned the only family I had left in the world for a childish fantasy. I thought of her face, pale and wrinkled and sagging, smiling and radiant and genial.

As if one could really make up for lost time, I said, "I'm coming over later. Around dinnertime."

"I'll prepare dinner," she said, her voice brightening.

I took my time, going to get a few of the ang ku kueh that she liked before visiting my favourite café. I had downed two coffees by the time I set off for home. When I arrived,

Grandma was standing at the small electric stovetop that she did all her cooking on these days. In the pot was her version of the Foochow dish red vinasse chicken. I once asked her if she could teach me how to cook it, but she refused. Maybe she wanted to keep her secrets, or maybe she thought that a guy should stay out of the kitchen. She could be traditional in that sort of way. Or maybe it was an insurance policy, to keep me by her side.

I put down my stuff in my room, then asked her if I could help. She just shooed me away. So, I took a look around the house. It felt as if time had been dilated or maybe intensified. I hadn't been away for that long, yet it felt like years.

I looked inside her room to see that everything was in its place. To one side of the room was the bed that belonged to Grandpa. He left us last year at the age of 93. For months they had been keeping an eye on a growth in his gut, certain that it would develop into a full-blown cancer, but in the end, it was a bout of pneumonia that claimed him. He spent his last weeks in the hospital, bedridden. At first, his condition was optimistic, but when he started to weaken, it happened rapidly, and before I knew it, he was on a mechanical respirator and couldn't even open his eyes.

The morning he left, we went to the hospital as soon as we got the phone call. Grandma didn't leave the car. She just stayed in the back of the taxi and cried silently. I can't remember what I said or who I met, but I remember seeing them cart him out on the gurney, covered in a white sheet. From there, the funerary services took over, and I just went along with whatever they suggested was best. The funeral was relatively quiet, all things considered. Grandpa never had many friends. He liked to keep to himself. Besides, he always said to me: "Being my age is like missing the bus that most of your friends have got on and having to wait for the next one."

After the funeral, we cleaned up the bed, but left it made, as if we were keeping the light on and expecting him to come home someday.

We had dinner at our small dining table, now made a little larger by Grandpa's absence. Grandma still kept a stool at the side that he used to sit. It may be a cliché to say so, but it was as though he had never really left. I spent the whole evening this way—distracted—and as my thoughts drifted, I looked up at the framed wedding photograph on the circuit breaker next to the main door, secured with a piece of raffia string. In that monochromatic picture, painted in shades that approximated breakfast tea, Grandpa and Grandma were garbed in Western wedding outfits, faces solemn. She was 16 at the time, and he was 18.

I had always wanted to ask her what it was like, what was going through her mind. Their marriage had been arranged by the parents, and they barely knew each other when the picture was taken. I wanted to ask if she was happy that day, but I wasn't sure that she would be able to remember a happiness from 75 or 80 years ago. And besides, with time, all memories distort and solidify, abandoning their original substance.

So, I kept my thoughts to myself. We ate in a type of peaceful quiet, the way we always did, and I went off shortly after the 10 pm news.

The next day, I found myself unable to work. Something had come over me, and it disturbed me that I couldn't quite figure out what it was. I put on music, I made a nice breakfast, I played a video game, but I felt uncomfortable, like a deep unrest had become dislodged and was beginning to metastasize within me.

I found momentary relief in chatting with my roommate. I sat down beside the ghost and told it about my life. I asked it what it was like to die, knowing full well that I would receive no answer. I told it that I didn't miss my parents all that much because the accident happened just before my fourth birthday and I never really got to know them. As a child, I loved those old-fashioned mango birthday cakes, I said.

I talked about Zigong and dinosaurs, and how my favourite dinosaur—the *Dimetrodon*—wasn't a dinosaur at all. I had a plastic toy of a *Dimetrodon* that could open its jaws if you pushed a button on the tail, and I used to make it chomp on my earlobes. I said to the ghost that I still have the toy today.

I asked if it knew my friend, and said that if it didn't, it would love her. She was the kindest person I knew. I mentioned that one time we were having dinner at a Korean restaurant and I had never seen edamame before in my life, so I ate the whole fibrous thing, pod and all. She must have noticed my poorly concealed and unusually aggressive chewing, but she never said a single word.

Through all my whining, the ghost kept quiet. It exuded a serenity that calmed me down as well. I wasn't sure that it understood anything that I said, but by the time I stopped, I realized that I had missed my dinner. I apologized for taking up its time and told it that I was going to get a shower and then head to bed.

I rang Grandma and she sounded as though she was crying. "What's wrong?" I asked. There was no answer. "I'm coming over now," I said, but she assured me that it was fine. She said that all my recent talk about ghosts made her dig up some photos, and there she saw her son and his wife.

"It's as though they're still here," she said. "No one is ever really gone." She went on to explain that what made her cry was the realization that they never got to know me, as though it was me who had been taken away from them.

The night rolled on. Red clouds had unfurled across the sky. Thunder rumbled. The wind was rising. I got up to close the windows but paused for a second—I loved the smell of rain.

We continued talking about the people who had left us. We didn't say anything that was especially revelatory, and neither of us learnt anything new. In fact, we had talked about these things before. But there was something about that conversation that was different, as though some invisible switch had been flipped, some unseen line crossed.

With the rain battering on the windows and the ghost watching silently from its corner, I slept soundly that night.

And then, Grandma had a stroke.

I was four months into the stay at my friend's place when it occurred. Things happened very quickly. There was the Incident, and then the Hospitalization, and then the Deterioration, and then the Silence, and then the Funeral, all within the span of three weeks. There were many people who came to see her off. She had been a very active and well-loved member of her congregation at church. Everyone expressed their sadness, but it all annoyed me because our grief was not the same. That is, they could never know the grandmother who raised me, the grandmother I lived with, the grandmother who faced her sadness with dignity. They just knew the woman who was devout and kind.

I was too shaken to handle the eulogy. Fortunately, one of the church leaders was said to be like a son to her and he was happy to take on the task. I just spent as much time as I could sitting in a corner by myself, away from the crowds, away from the voices. I didn't want to talk. However, some relatives from Malaysia that I didn't recognize came to greet me and offer their sympathies. I tried to keep myself from breaking down. One of them, a distant cousin, handed me a photograph of Grandma. She said that they had found it at home before coming down. I thanked her.

In the photo, Grandma looked like she was in her fifties. She wore tinted glasses and a white hat. My teenage father stood next to her. Something about it disturbed me and, not wanting to have to deal with it then, I slotted the photo into my diary.

On the third day of proceedings, I watched as her remains were sent into the incinerator on a motor-driven cart. Around me, there was a lot of weeping. One of the men from the church had brought a guitar into the observation area, and midway through proceedings, he roused the weeping crowd into a Mandarin rendition of *Amazing Grace*. The loudness of the chorus felt at odds with what was happening, but I didn't mind. I think Grandma would have appreciated it. She would sometimes put on hymns on the old cassette player if she had trouble sleeping.

And then, after the song, after the funeral, there was just unbearable silence.

For the next week, I didn't leave the house. I barely even left the room. I couldn't bring myself to. There were a lot of tears, and also fear—inexplicable fear, overbearing, awful. I was scared to even go to the bathroom. The world trembled every time I stepped out of the bed. I kept the lights off at all times. I slept very little. I ate even less. I ignored my need for food for as long as I could and almost convinced myself not to buy any groceries. But I knew it wasn't what Grandma would have wanted, so I just ordered them online and someone left them outside the door.

I thought about returning home instead of staying at my friend's, but I wasn't ready to face the space that she used to inhabit. Besides, at least I wasn't alone here. Through it all, the ghost was a silent witness, giving me the space to grieve, indulging my unexplainable fear of the world.

One night, I looked at that photo of Grandma with the aid of the glow from my phone. It felt brittle in my hand. I noticed how different her smile was back then. Then I put it down. Something about it provoked a violent reaction in me. I felt sick.

Suddenly it occurred to me that I hadn't said a single word in a whole week. So, as scared as I was, I crawled out of the sheets, photograph in hand, and sidled up next to the ghost. Leaning back against the wall, I sat on the floor, staring at it. Minutes passed. It almost seemed to be waiting patiently for me. When I could finally summon the words, I said, my voice cracking, "Another one. I'm all alone now."

The tears were relentless. With great effort, I placed the photo on the floor, right next to the ghost. I didn't want to touch it again. She was gone, I thought. Gone. And the photograph was a grotesque reminder of my new reality.

I limped back to bed and cried until I could fall asleep.

I woke with a start in the middle of the night. Next to me on the bed, bent over and staring at me in the darkness, was the ghost. We looked at each other for moments. It felt like our eyes met even though it didn't have any. Then it made a noise I had never heard it make before, a soft humming, like a mother hushing her child to sleep. And then it moved. I couldn't see it clearly in the dark and without my glasses, but it almost looked like it had a hand, and it was holding something.

It placed the object on my chest. By the time I found my glasses, it had turned its back towards me and was shuffling away. The object was the photograph of Grandma. After weeks and weeks of a type of grossly limited communication, this was its first real message to me. And as I looked at the photograph, familiar words echoed in my mind, *No one is ever really gone.*

I held onto the photograph and looked up at the ghost again. Sluggishly, it retreated to its corner, and then, as if it had finally said what it had waited months to say, it slowly dissolved into the darkness. It never returned.

ROMANCES

Genericity of Rejections

Hey

Thank you for telling me this

It's very brave and I'm touched

but I'm sorry

I don't feel the same way about you

Hi

I'm not as good as you say

You deserve someone better

I understand

I wish you all the best, ok?

I'm sorry for being a bother

I'll get out of your way now

No, you aren't a bother

It's not like that

Sorry for everything

Hey

Please stop saying sorry

Sure

You are a great guy

and I'm sure you'll find someone

to treasure you

lol

Don't tell me what to do

Don't be like that

I really wish you all the best

Best wishes

That's not what that means

Best regards

What does that even mean?

True

What does it mean

Are you making fun of me
But
yes what does it

Sorry again

Sorry yourself
Your sorry self

Apply coupon code

SORRY15

to your next purchase

Thank you for shopping with us

                    Thank you for your participation

Thank you for not smoking

                         Thank you for smoking

You're welcome

                            welcome to
                            bienvenue
                         selamat datang
                          wilkommen
                            歡迎光臨

These things they say all the time
These things we say all the time

                             yeah
                             like
                  there are plenty of fish in the sea

Like time heals all wounds

           you should never judge a book by its cover

But first impressions count

                      love at first sight

Love is blind

                         love sucks

Yeah
I know
the most useless word

                      toni morrison?

What?
Ok
Anyway
I really wish you all the best

sure

By the way

where do I use that coupon code?

Love Letter

<u>Usage Instructions</u>

<u>You will need:</u>

1. The following pages.
2. Access to a photocopier or some means to make a copy of the pages.
3. A pair of scissors or a craft knife with a ruler.
4. An empty envelope.

<u>Directions</u>

1. Photocopy the next pages.
2. Cut out each segment of text/paragraph to produce 10 strips of paper.
3. Fold each strip into a small square, approximately 1cm in width.
4. Place the 10 strips of paper in the envelope.
5. Shuffle the pieces within the envelope and draw one piece out. Unfold it and read.
6. Repeat step 5 until satisfied.

On the first day, he is giddy with anticipation after posting the letter. He cannot wait for a reply. He is nervous, but glad most of all that he has found the courage to profess his feelings.

On the third day, he wonders how she will send her reply. That is, will she write back? Will she call him? Or will she simply text him?

Fifth day: He supposes that patience is a virtue. Postage services take time, he reminds himself.

Sixth day: He starts to think that it was a bad idea to write a letter. Who writes a letter in this day and age? She must think he is so old-fashioned. A curio, not a lover.

Seventh: Why *did* he write a letter? Everything rests on the letter. A judgement of his ability to express himself.

On the ninth day, he thinks that nothing depends on the letter. That in the end, his words do not matter, and certainly not his feelings. Nothing matters.

Day 10: He anxiously wonders why she has yet to reply. Did it get lost? Of course he shouldn't have trusted the postal service!

Day 13: He begins to imagine her response. He knows that it will fall into the common trappings of romance. "You deserve someone better." Something like that. He doesn't understand why he wants an answer despite knowing that it will be drawn from the realm of cliché. Perhaps he too is cliché waiting for cliché.

On the 15th day, he knows it is all one big mistake. He should never have sent anything.

23rd day: A mess of tears.

Comedy

I need to say something. No, something needs to be said. That's more like it. I was told by the voice in my head, or maybe that was me, and this is just the voice in my head speaking. We're all voices in someone's head, after all. Where am I, I forget. You must forgive me if I seem slipshod, haphazard, substandard. It's usually because I'm very forgetful. It's the first thing I tell everyone. Yes. Well, that's not the first thing I told you, no, but by the time I started that sentence, it was too late. Time is always irretrievable. We should just be allowed to go back, but that might be too much, too much. And here we are, here I am, talking. Sure, I'm talking to myself. Well, I'm talking to you, but the thing is, only you would know that when it happens, if it happens. As for me, I can only guess. How do I talk to myself anyway? Have you ever wondered? You must have wondered about that at some point in time. Questions, simple questions. Existentialist questions, as the brainiacs will tell you. A lot of people obsess over these things, let me tell you that. Once, I had a roommate who spent all his time thinking about it. *God doesn't exist*, he said, and he looked so sad. I asked him why he looked so sad, and he just shrugged, and there was the look of nothing in his eyes. Then I asked why he was here, why any one of us was here, and he shrugged again. *I can't find it within myself*, he said. Two weeks later, he killed himself, that poor sod. God bless his soul. He had something of a point though, that it's hard to find anything within ourselves. What's the kernel, the seed, the bloody and beating heart, and what's the shell, the hollow, the cradle and the grave? I tend to think that this me that you see here is the picture, the stage voice, the persona. Like the colours and lines of a cubist painting assembled in disarray. A frail and nervous shape. A gentle contradiction. This is myself, but not my *self*. And this self really isn't all that important, is it? Compared to what we want to be seen as, the image that we try to identify our selves as, because that's the only one we really know, and that's the only one anyone will ever know. Maybe there is no self hidden beneath all of these contraptions and we're all just counterfeiters. I went to a priest one day and I told him, you know what, God made us all to be liars. He was troubled, so troubled—his face told me so. He must have thought it an unmentionable, and I felt ashamed, so I quickly left and never went back to that congregation again. I still wonder from time to time if he knew what I meant. More usually, however, I wonder if I know what I meant. Maybe it was really me, the real me, speaking. Or, maybe I told him that just to change how he saw me, just to disturb the balance, because if you don't disturb things in balance, you'd never know you were alive. Yeah, maybe I was lying, just to make things uncomfortable. Comfort, continuity, changelessness, these things lull us into sleep, and quietly our souls drift away with the wind. I'm drifting now, aren't I? I've strayed from my original intent, if I had one, though I forget. Maybe I'm just here talking to myself, or to my self. It's hard to tell sometimes. I don't know what the self is, the actual me, the objective me. And I'm back to this again. It's a bloody circle, isn't it? Is this what they call "circular reasoning"? Or maybe, and this just occurred to me, I'm not doing anything in particular. I'm just fucking around. My ma told me once that we're all here to fuck around. No not my ma, maybe pa, maybe I told myself that. Doesn't matter. Ma, pa, me, all the same. People are not so different from one another once you get used to them. At first you think that the more you know them, the more different they become to you, but that's just a trick; the more you know them, the more you realize how much you don't know about them. Believe me if you don't know already, what you know is nothing compared to what you don't know. Anyway, they all become the same in the vastness of their unknowability. When I was very young, oh, forgive me, I just thought I'd change things up a bit to keep it interesting. When I was very young, my ma told me about the story of gentle Abraham, who had been asked to kill his son on a mountain as a sacrifice to God—the Binding of Isaac, it was called. You think that he must have struggled out of love for his son, but perhaps his love of god was greater, and he found the resolve to lead his son up the mountain and just as he was about to go through with the act, an angel stopped him, and Abraham was rewarded for his obedience. When I was older, I'd always imagined that both Abraham and Isaac, son of Abraham, would have to live with this for the rest of their lives. Because, if you think about it, as soon as Abraham had made up his mind to complete the sacrifice, the act was finished. I mean, Isaac survived, but he was also dead. Thoughts and actions and the action of thought, all irreversible. And Abraham, poor gentle Abraham, like the victim of a practical joke, could never face his son again, never love his son again. What an awful existence. Would it have been as bad if Abraham had been allowed to kill his son physically? What was God thinking? Oh dear, an unmentionable. Forgive me. Let's talk about something else. Let's talk about love. I fell in love once, well, more than once, but I mean, this one time. She was this lovely creature with eyes that looked like the edge of spring, skin that tingled with impossible energy, and lips that . . . oh, I don't know but I think I'm getting carried away. The loveliest creature, let's leave it at that, and I was the hopeless, hapless dog grovelling at her feet. She was with someone else, though. I had never met him, never seen them together, so to be fair, maybe he didn't exist. But I knew what I knew because other people told me about it, and she strongly suggested it to me once. It didn't stop me from caring for her, doing things for her, and so on; this went on for years. And I discovered that as long as I kept the romantic gestures little, well, she didn't mind those. She must have thought I was a very good friend who liked doing things and giving things, but then again, she must have known that I was still crazy about her, so I'm not sure. I get confused sometimes. Anyway, I was so tormented over it. She didn't do anything, really, but somehow she changed my whole life. I reckon that she could have actually done something about it, but she didn't, she just let it be. And sometimes I wonder how differently things would have turned out if she had taken some sort of action, but it probably wouldn't have been too different from this. So I don't blame her, no. After all, that's how it is with everything in life, isn't it? Damned if you do, damned if you don't. A choiceless choice, a nonchoice. You're basically fucked. But I wanted to say that she destroyed my capacity for romance. I tried to move on, because that's what everyone says you should do, but I couldn't. She gradually eroded my faculties of romance, and at one point, I realized that I just couldn't love again. I mean, I tried. There were three of them. Two other girls and a boy. No, four of them, another boy, just to even the numbers out. To be frank, I could have just made that last one up and you would be none the wiser, unless, of course, I'm talking to myself, at which point I would be lying to myself. But lying to yourself is impossible anyway, if you think about it. I don't know who invented that expression. Yes, yes, I know what you're thinking now, that I've loved both boys and girls. Don't tell anyone.

Please. People are very strict about these things, about love, about divisions, especially in the congregations, among the thoushaltnots. Sometimes I tell myself that I don't know what the fuss is all about, or maybe the Father told me and I forgot. It's all love, isn't it? And sometimes, a thought occurs to me, like so, why can't men have babies, in the fashion of any other thought occurring to me, like so, why can't dogs wear ties? It's all just love, and there shouldn't be divisions, and no one ever got hurt by a thought, I think, but what do I know? And here's another thought coming, like so, why is the Christian god a father, the Father? I say this not out of disrespect for all your other religions; it's not that I don't want to pay attention to them, it's just that this is the only one that I know or remember. Why does God have to be male. Oh heresies, I've outdone myself this time. Unmentionable upon unmentionable. It makes sense, nevertheless, though the serpent made a lot of sense too, but let's not digress. Why should God have to choose anyway, or are we too harebrained, scatterbrained, to think outside of our nervous dichotomies, so much so that God has to choose for us? Am I blaspheming, please pray, please, pretty please tell me if I'm blaspheming again? It's not deliberate, more out of habit, no, what am I saying, out of habit. Imagine that, blaspheming out of habit. Maybe I can't help it. I hope I haven't offended Him. Him, there's something wrong about that word, something that disturbs me, because, I think, of the way it sounds. Try saying it, utter it like you mean it. See how it makes you press your lips together, stops any sound any breath from leaving your lips, that ending sound, that authoritative 'm'. It wants to be its own word, won't let you take charge of it. Possessive, in charge, just like how we imagine men to be, though most of them are not like that, and I despise the ones who are. Compare that to 'her', with its openness, fluidity, possibilities, the ease with which it moves, transforms, joins another word, suggests nothingness or somethingness. Far cry from 'him'. And don't tell me about 'his'. His is just the sound a snake makes when it makes any sound at all. Makes you wonder why it's hers but not hims. I guess it's because hims would just sound like we were talking about going to church, though, come to think of it, religion is not usually that far removed from possession and masculinity. He doesn't end like that, but that's only because it's taken out of she like man was taken out of woman, like Eve was taken out of Adam. Most men are removed from women in the first place. The point is, I made up my mind not to be either. I don't want to feel like a man or like a woman. I'm just a person, or not even that. A person is just a word anyway, or is it the other way around? But you do know that she wasn't the only one, don't you? Eve, I mean. There was good old Lilith, god bless her soul, made out of clay, not out of Adam. She wasn't subservient enough, so she got banished, serves her right. Anyway, I wanted to tell you this story that someone told me when I was a child, maybe. There was a king and he had twelve sons. One day, he sends all of them out, asking that they come back with brides to be. They go off on their horses, this dirty dozen, but the youngest one gets left behind not long after because his older brothers feel that he is useless. This youngest prince is powerless to resist the influence or perhaps the physiques of his elder brothers and gets left behind. What's a man to do, deserted by his cruel brothers? He wanders around until he comes across a doll lying in the middle of nowhere. Or perhaps I misremember, and a little girl asks him to visit a doll lying in the middle of nowhere. In the grass. The young prince tells the doll, the littlest doll, Hello, how do you do? My brothers have left me here and for some odd reason that means I can't continue on my quest to find my bride to be, but you're beautiful, you're gorgeous, and you will be my wife. He doesn't even ask, doesn't say please. The doll is all too delighted to make him a shirt, which is too small, and it reminds our prince that she, too, is too small. This is extremely troubling to him, but on their way back to see the king, an accident occurs. The doll ends up in a pond or a river, it doesn't matter, all bodies of water are the same once you get used to them. The prince is horrified. Thankfully, a merman is on hand to rescue her. Now the prince is thrilled. The littlest of dolls, it seems, is now bloated to just the right size. They return to the king just as the eleven brothers return, but their human wives are too headstrong, too stubborn, too indomitable. You see, they've been fighting during the entire journey to the palace, out of jealousy, you imagine. So they're now ugly. No one wants ugly wives. The king will have none of this. He chases all of them away and celebrates the wedding of his youngest son. The end. What a horrific story. Only the men get to do anything in there, and the best of the women just happens to be a doll. And not just any doll, but a sponge, just waiting to absorb and receive all your sweat, your tears, your precious secretions. The independent women, on the other hand, end up ugly and get their just desserts; serves them right. I won't stand for this. I don't want to be like them, the men, the princes of the world. I don't want to be like the women either, doomed and ugly/pretty. I just want to be myself. And I wonder, just sometimes I wonder, how courage works, along with heroism, and romance; it's all wrong, games of perverts. Art too. You don't see how aberrant it's become. Let me tell you what real art is. Real art is a struggle, a climb up a peculiarly difficult staircase. Real art is a contradiction, like real love, because you can never achieve what you set out to achieve, but the means are the ends in themselves. If you could succeed, then there wouldn't be a point in the continued existence of art, real art. And I also think that real art shows no respect if it doesn't have to. To words, to language, to pictures, to images, to people, to God. Oh dear it seems that real art is responsible for mentioning unmentionables too. But it's true, art should be barefaced, stark naked, because it has to cut to the bone and crush all our measly little hearts. Actually, I can't tell you what real art is. What do I know anyway? And I've run out of things to say, so I had better go back. There were two other girls and two boys, as I was saying. I tried romance, I tried to pursue them, or I tried things out with them, et cetera. The first girl was short, I remember. She wore her hair in curls, and had these plump, pink lips. She ignored me as best she could. And anyway, eventually I thought that she was just a distraction. The first boy, well, let's not talk about him, I'd rather not talk about him. He was a mistake, just like the rest of us. The second boy was tall and had these slender fingers like a pianist's or a catburglar's. He was sweet, but it just felt nothing like what I knew to be love. The second girl was beautiful for her assertiveness, her charisma, and her smile, but I was suspicious of taking a liking to her. Nevertheless, I persisted in my needless needy fidelity. And then I knew that I would always be true, and it meant that I would really be miserable, but being miserable is better than being vacuous and mute. It's fine to be miserable. I always tell my friends that it's okay not to be happy, it's fine to be depressed. I knew and know plenty of depressed people, angry people, and they all thrive along the same equators of madness. But all of these friends look at me like I've gone off my rocker. I haven't, you know. Who said that happiness has to be the foundation of a good life, and who said that life has any right to be good anyway? We should be just as satisfied with our life of agonies as we are with our life of glees, or we shouldn't be satisfied at all. It's all shit, anyway. But all of that romance, it was all a game, really, and it never felt the same again after I fell for her, the first one I was talking about. But you should know that love's a fragile thing, and let me tell you,

I did my best to protect it. All of the people told me things I didn't want to hear, but I don't blame them because they've always meant well. Some of them said that she was using me, and that was fine, because I loved her. Some of them said that I was being impractical, and that was true, though I couldn't understand it. But that's the way love is. It's like religion, which is impractical and relies on a certain ignorance, probably because it entails a precious love. Really nothing else avails us, so we make do, as we make do with love. Speaking of which, I had a friend once, and that's just a manner of speaking, because that wasn't the only time I had a friend, and I still have that friend. Or I think I still do. Anyway, he, she, what does it matter, fell in love. It happened so suddenly, he, she, it said, and they were together and happy for a bit until I received a letter that told me it was over, giving no explanation at all, and that, I must add, was very clearly stated, that there was no particular reason at all. My friend said that it was difficult to accept at first, but then thought that nothing ever happens for any particular reason anyway. It was not what I imagined, said it, she, he. But nothing is ever as we imagine anyway, so I don't know why we bother. Maybe we can't help ourselves. As we all know, love is troublesome. The thing that gets to me, though, is that I wouldn't really have cared if I hadn't, that is, if I hadn't cared. I wouldn't have been hurt, disappointed, upset, because I couldn't have been, but I was, and there was really very little that anyone could have done about it because it was too late by that time; it's always too late. But again, love is troublesome. I had trouble coming to terms with this particular romance, until one day I realized that the only way out of it was not to have started in the first place; but you only say that when it's too late, and it's always too late. That was when I accepted that I would never love again. But what does it matter if you can't love, can't fall in love, can't fall out of love? Life carries on. We go on, you and I. We go on. Especially me, both the metaphorical me and the real me. But the real me, too, is a metaphor for the real me, which, too, is a metaphor, and it goes on and on, as we go on and on. I hate metaphors, but the nature of words is infuriating because they prevent you from saying exactly what you mean, because all words are metaphors at some level. It is a ridiculous enterprise, really. You can't choose to say precisely what you mean to say. Our grotesque lack of choice, this. It's awful. And then you think about it and you wonder if you ever really know what you mean, because it's plain to see that we all think with words, too. God, what a cop out. Fuck I've done it again, another unmentionable. I don't know who keeps putting these thoughts and expressions in my head. And then, just then, another thought occurs to me, like so: what do words really mean, or what does each word really mean? Funny to think of it, how we usually define words with other words, and how we describe things with words, because things are so many things at one time and words are so few, so few. There's something insidious about the way they skirt around the central issue, the central thingness, the central beingness, so completely complicit in our common delusional denomination. Words are always metaphorical, representational, our means of assuming our places in this wild, wordless world. They're removed from anything they describe, and thus, they remove us from what they describe too. Always, always at a distance, too distant, too far. Spooky action at a distance. Words destroy reality, negate reality. I mean I— wait, that's rich. Can I mean anything at all? It's all just approximations, isn't it? And is that good enough? It really messes with your head. If you can't mean what you want to mean, what about meaning, where do you find it, and what do you do with it? The way I see it, meaning isn't an object, or a noun as those brainy academic sorts put it. It's a process in motion, like skiing, or barfing, or fucking. Fucking is all about love, don't let anyone tell you any different, and the thing is that I never saw very much wrong with fucking. Sure beats the hell out of fighting, killing, proselytizing, blaspheming, though I do that sometimes. In any case, meaning is a continuous action. Just like I am meaning right now, in the process called meaning. That's frightening because it implies that there was nothing to begin with, but I can't complain. I mean, what other world can I know? And anyway, I think it's time to shuffle the pack to make things interesting again. So let me just say that I know what you're thinking. Or maybe if this is just me talking to myself, then I know what I'm thinking, which doesn't happen very often. That's a postmodernist if I ever saw one. But that's not true because I'm not familiar with the term, it's something those brainy scholarly types use, and I can scarcely imagine what it means. My friend says that a postmodernist comes after the modernist, which made me realize that the postman must surely be the most biologically advanced animal on earth. Also, you could be thinking, oh you philosopher. And that wouldn't be true too because I don't have a license. In fact, I believe that everyone thinks of these things as long as they want to live. So no, I'm not a philosopher, a thinker, I resent that word. Call me a writer. Call me a songwriter. Or a scrivener, a gravedigger, a maneater, a sadist, a turnip, a poet, a little boy with a polka dot skirt. But it's not true, I couldn't be any one of those possibilities, I'm not any one possibility. Don't be mistaken. I sometimes wonder if God makes mistakes. Maybe we're God's mistakes, and the thing is we'd be none the wiser, see. Oh there we go, another unmentionable. I should really just throw in the towel now. I should give up religion, if I haven't already, I don't remember, but I think it's clear that I'm not very good at it. Come to think of it, does anyone really ever get good at religion? I don't think so, but maybe thinking's the problem. Thinking's a disease. I once read a book about a man whose disease was thinking. He just kept thinking his way through things and that made him ignorant, incorrigible, and inert. He lost his wife, mind you, because of this disease. I remember that very well. What I'm not so sure of is whether or not it was a book. It could have been a movie, could have been a friend. Doesn't matter, all stories. Anyway, thinking. It's so much like speaking, because as soon as you start thinking, you start inventing, and that's no way to live, so let's just stop thinking. But thinking is like speaking, writing. Perhaps I should say nothing. I should keep quiet. Maybe that's what that falseness inside of me is. It's just words. Maybe it's all one big fat lie and there's no truth to get to. Words are the instrument of the Devil after all. And God, why, he's the opposite, of course. God has silence. Silence, it is the only thing that marks the passing of the hour. Has the universe ever gone quiet for you? Has the sea ever gone quiet for you? Have you ever noticed how quiet the sun is? I'll shut up now, I really will, but I just wanted to say that we should stay away from the words if they are the tools of the Devil, and maybe, we should aspire to silence. No, we must not aspire to godhood. Or is it god. They always say that you shouldn't be as presumptuous as to hope to impress upon your image the likeness of God, or that of any divine being. It's human arrogance, and an aspect of our hearts of darkness. I've thought of this before, and I once asked, *then how am I supposed to know what to be, how do I know what I am supposed to live like, what am I meant to aspire to?* But as soon as the words left my mouth, I realized that I'd just mentioned another unmentionable. But you can never take your words back. Anyone who says, I take my words back, is bloody lying. So anyway, I learnt that I couldn't love anymore. Oh, I've come back to this again. I also wanted to add that I've learnt that the only consistent outcome of love is pain. Someone told me that once, but I can't remember, or remember wrongly, or simply don't know if I remember correctly. As you can tell, not knowing is worse than remembering wrongly, because it drives you crazy. You should always be able to be certain of things, but there's so little in life you can be sure of; that's a pretty dreadful way to live. But think about it, the only consistent outcome of love is pain. People break up, people get old, people change, and people die. The truth is, if you have nothing to lose, you're goddamn invincible. Love is so troublesome. I've already said that, haven't I? I'm very forgetful. Doesn't hurt to say anything twice, or at least, not as much as it could for not saying it at all. But I'll bore you, if I haven't already, and I'll bore myself. Let me tell you a story instead. I once chopped down a tree in school. It was a young sapling of a sort, and I was ten or twelve and did it for my own reasons. Maybe it was the temptation of the axe, and the temptation of destruction, and the temptation of doing something I had never done before. It was school property, of course, and the discipline master was quickly on the case. He must have thought that I did it to spite the school, and maybe that was true, but it wasn't to me. So I told him what I had done and why I had done it—to the best of my ability—but he wasn't satisfied. Tell the truth, he said, but I was so confused because I didn't know if he wanted his truth or if my truth was not satisfactorily described, and I didn't want to guess. There were words that he wanted to hear and words that I wanted to say, and in the infinite sea of possibilities, what were the chances that they would be the same words. It's the same with every question and every demand that they make out of you, the teachers, the friends, the police. Is this what they know as irreconcilable difference, I can't be sure, but you should have seen us fools, standing there, trying to come to an agreement, when we were handicapped right from the start. Did we have to be? Speaking of trees, you know that old saying, or maybe the old joke, I forget, that says, if a tree falls in the forest and no one is there to hear it, does it make a sound? It's supposed to be some philosophical question, the possibility of something that isn't seen or heard or smelled or felt or tasted existing. Frightening thing, because it leaves us at the mercy of others, that is, I can never by my own efforts make myself be. What good is being and meaning if we can never master them ourselves, I wonder? Someone may have explained it to me once, but I can't remember. Really, though, what's the difference between remembering and knowing? My ma used to tell me that you're only as good as what you know, no, what you remember. I don't remember her exact words, I should weep. Although to think of it, what can you really know. I mean, really. Tell me, what do you know? I've asked you a question that you shouldn't be able to answer. I've thought my way into a corner now, haven't I? And that's why I think thinking's a disease. Anyway, where was I? Where am I? What am I saying? Oh, that you can't really know anything. In knowing something, you know it utterly, and that's the gift of God, though I think I'm using that in the wrong way, misappropriations. What would life be without misunderstandings, misapproximations, misappropriations? But you get what I mean. Knowledge is an instrument of power. We're not allowed it. It's okay. It doesn't offer us dominion, or purpose, or sense. Knowing's for God, gods, whatever you will. That's their work, and we're the farthest things from gods, I kid you not, like opposites, we are. That said, I sure would like to know who the hell I am. It's like an itch you can't reach. Well, not exactly, but that'll do, that'll have to do. I think the point I was trying to get at, actually, is that knowledge fails like memory fails, so maybe they're the same thing, or at least related. Memories are imperfect, that's the way they're made. As soon as you try to recall anything, you idealize and criticize, you cherish, you recompense, and sometimes you just make stuff up. I remember, for instance, this man who's completely mad, epitome of madness, he got really good at it, talked about the time of waste and the tether of the end, and once he said to me that he would swallow me whole if I didn't run, and I didn't, but that's only because he's mad. Anyway, the important thing is, I don't remember whether he was a friend, an enemy, a relative, a character from one of those moldy old storybooks on those moldy old shelves, or an imagining that I should be proud of. But you see, memory is a lot like getting to know people. We trust in our capacity to know them, just as we trust in our memories, when you and I know too well that it's all just a bundle of incompleteness. And then, we say things about them the same way we judge reality through our memories, through our veil of halfknowing and notknowing. It's a little presumptuous, don't you think? No, sorry, don't think, leave the thinking to me, I can't help myself. Now and then I remember ma, dear ma, memories of her, no that's not a pun, but there's no way of ever knowing if what I remember of her is what she actually spent her time being. I can see her face in the puffy clouds of my mind but how could I ever know if I've understated, exaggerated, underexaggerated all of the terrestrial features of that brilliant shape. I can see her, so plump, no, fat, no, enormous; her magnificent girth testing the borders of this imagined space. Then I realize how enormous, too, those letters have become, not quite capital letters, like MA, but close enough. You have to wonder, though, if there's any difference between what I know and what I remember, or if they enhance one another, or impair one another, or deceive one another. I don't know. Logically, the same could be said about so much else in our lives; since remembrance is not dependable and not to be trusted, we shouldn't depend on it, but that's easy to say, as most things are. I've nothing else to depend on. And I don't want to let go, I never want to let go, all of these accumulations, flagrant though their falseness may be. If I surrendered these shams of mine, it's possible, completely possible, that I would have nothing left, and I'm scared of nothing. Besides, God didn't make us to be instantaneous creatures. Living is the impossible tedium of trying to come up with the truth by making up a bunch of lies. Oh I should shut up, I should leave this to the stuffy, brainy types and their brain stuff, I should. The more I talk the more confused I become, the more scared I get, but eventually I just keep going, so I must be crazy, at least a little bit. Everyone's a little crazy, though, if everyone's a little crazy, then no one's really a little crazy at all. That might be all I am, a dash of craziness and nothing else, but it's not like I chose to be like that. You can't blame me for my nature. And that too disturbs me. Do I get a choice of what I am to be, am I allowed to pick, to alter, to redefine? Mind you, I didn't choose to get born and I didn't choose to exist, this is so unfair. And then you think, at some level, I can choose, like I chose with the priest. My choice of demeanour, my choice of words, but that's just who I pretend to be, and that's who I never actually am. Why would I want to live a life like that? Why would anyone. We don't happen by choice, at least, not our own, little more than accidents. It's a mockery, effrontery, comedy. Don't know the word for it. Words fail me. I hate words, they're good for nothing. Words imprison you, make you say things that you don't exactly mean; I've said that before, but I'll say it again. Of course the logical thing is to avoid words completely then, but how else could I speak? And don't tell me about pictures, they work the same. Sometimes, when I'm feeling brave, I ask, *how is it that I cannot help saying things when I'm not meant to say things? How do I live when there is so much I can say, but so little that I can mean?* Oh dear, I keep going round in circles, or keep going back. Time to change things up again. I had a dream once, let me tell you, and I was married, with that girl I was telling you about, and we had children, two of them, our flesh and blood, maybe, adopted, maybe. And she woke me up and asked if I was going to take the kids to school, and so on. The day went by, and we spent our time in our standard-issue family lives. It was striking how real all of it was. After I woke, I knew that I had imagined it involuntarily, and that it wasn't true. But what did I know that was true anyway? Maybe it's just that, we've all imagined our own ideal realities and realnesses. Maybe we've been hoodwinked into believing that seeing is being, the grand deception of our ideas. So what we're really chasing after, here, now, there, then, everywhere, everywhen, is nothing but a preconception, no less false than the imaginings of our dreams and the inventions of our words. Look, look at me, all of these words and I still don't have the foggiest idea who I am, what I am, where I am. What am I? Person, creature, thing. Yes, thing, that sounds most like it, and yet nothing like it. I am a persona, a Pierrot, a plastic soul. I am a wreck, a lost child. I am a voice waiting to be wrestled into the sea of silence. And yet I am not any of these things. I am not what I am. I am not I. That's like a game. I used to play this game with anagrams, so I got pretty good with anagrams. If you don't know, an anagram is when you rearrange letters to make a new word, like being and binge, words and sword, mean and amen, and all this shit. I always think that there must be some relationship between a word and its anagram, some mysterious coincidence or accidental catastrophe. Or maybe it is a way of words trying to come to terms with themselves, choosing the arrangement of letters, moving towards some semblance of honesty. By the way, the only anagram for I is I. As far as variety goes, that's a real embarrassment of riches. Anyway, we shouldn't take games so seriously, it was just a thought. I should shut up now. I had wanted to earlier on, but things never go according to plan. I think we make them just because there's nothing better to do. I had a son once. Oh, I'm sorry, I should have said this sooner! But things never occur to me in the right order as they do in those novels, novellas, novellettes. Life is nothing like the books, and yet, we can't keep ourselves from them. I suppose it's because life is exactly like the books, and it's just a heap of lies. Anyway, I was saying, I had a son, and I had made all of these plans for him, hopes and dreams, but everything gets derailed as soon as you start. It's the nature of things, spiralling out of control. Everything's an accident waiting to happen, and it never quite worked out for my son. I wish I could say that it was my fault, that I could have done better, but now that I think of it, I couldn't have done any better, except to not have made plans, not to have had a son in the first place. It's not my fault, and it wasn't yours either, my son. Oh what a dreary thing to be thinking about. Let me change the topic again, just once more, one last time. I'm going to tell you, if you're still listening, still reading, still perceiving, about this girl I fell in love with. She destroyed my capacity for romance and—oh, damn, I've done this already, haven't I? I may have even done it more than once. Is rerepeating all I'm ever good at doing? I should shut up now. I should stop. You'd think it'd be easy when there's so little I can actually say, but what do you know, but I'm finishing now. And when it's over, there will be silence and then I will say that it is finished. Someone said that once. Who said that? What's finished? Nothing's finished, nothing's ever finished, nothing begins. I think I'll just tie up a few loose ends, as they say, in order to give the illusion of completeness, in order to lull myself into rest. There's something so nauseatingly vexing about it, though, how I keep saying that I will stop when it's just the thing that's preventing me from stopping. It's because, I think, an idea is designed to be unattainable, so in a sense, to want something is to be unable to get it. Life's horrible, but I've known that ever since I was introduced to it. Still, I should stop, even if I can never stop thinking, expressing, lying. I can never, because once you know the words, you can never unknow them. They become your tendency, your compulsion. They become you. No, let's not digress. Loose ends, yes. I never saw the girl again, for one thing. I might in the future, who knows, but I'm not making any plans to. I didn't go back to see the priest. I'm still ashamed. And ma and pa, god bless their souls. I hope I've done them proud, I really do. And my son. Yes, I had a son, and it was really all an accident. Nevertheless, I won't hesitate to say that he was the most precious thing, and for a moment I thought that I had found the meaning of my life. I abhorred that suggestion later because I realized it meant that I lived for him, and it made me vomit; well, I didn't literally vomit. To think that I had always been living for something else, someone else . . . Then I thought, and thinking's a disease, that ma had always lived for me. And then I realized that I had signed for him, I had birthed him into his life of debt, and I asked, my son, *my son, what have I done?* Everything just came together at that point in time, like it was a puzzle that I had spent all the years of my parenthood trying to assemble. So I put my hands around his pale, skinny neck, and my fingers felt the solidness of his throat, my palms the hollows of his shoulders. He was looking at me as if he was searching for the words, the language to express himself, and when he failed, those eyes watered. And I was gentle Abraham, and I was mother Medea, and I strangled him, I strangled him dead. His eyes closed. He never looked more at peace. He was gone, and my task was done. Maybe I will have children again, in the future, or maybe I won't. No plans. But again, let's not digress. At that moment, I knew I had done the right thing, the just thing, and I knew that he knew too, but I couldn't understand why my face was wet. I let go of his neck and cradled him in my arms, his head lolling, his limbs dangling. *I've strangled him, I've strangled him dead*, I said aloud to myself, but I couldn't hear my own voice. The only sound in my ears was the incomprehensible silence, and I couldn't tell if that was horrific or reassuring, because I knew that my nature was words. You see, it's too late for us now, it always has been. It's too late for me now, and I will never know the silence. And maybe I can stop here, or maybe I can't.

VISIONS

Bloom

When Louis woke up that morning, he opened three eyes.

He didn't realize this at first, although certainly it was unusual that his vision was blurred. He rubbed at his two old ones to no avail. It felt as if he had tried and failed to scratch an itch. But as he did so, he brushed against a mysterious lump on his forehead that he discovered was capable of blinking.

Disoriented and confused, he didn't dare move. Naturally, there was a great temptation to believe that he was merely dreaming, so he tried to get back to sleep. But with each passing second that he failed to do so, his new eye slipped more and more into reality, until he reached a point at which he could no longer deny its permanence. Louis panicked.

He turned his head quickly to check if his wife was still in bed; she wasn't. She was probably downstairs tending to their son, born a year ago. Fifteen months, to be more precise. Louis was never any good with children. Once, when watching his child at play among his toys, Louis was paralysed by an inexplicable sense of trepidation. Perhaps it was the thought that his son, just one month old at the time, still had so much of his life ahead of him, or that Louis had lived far too much of his, but the new father was unable to move from his chair. This non-interaction persisted for several weeks until, eventually, Louis decided that it simply wasn't working for him. Louis loved his son, no doubt, but he found that he had to assure himself of that fact constantly. In fact, that the child had yet to begin walking, was a constant source of distress for Louis. It was just that perhaps he had lost all sense of what it was to be a child, and therefore, had no sense of how to be a parent.

Louis stumbled out of bed. You might be surprised to learn that he did not see better with a third eye, which is 50% more eye than most humans, but it makes sense when one takes some time to think about it. It's just physics. He struggled to think of any creatures, big or small, with an odd number of eyes.

Carefully making sure he didn't kick any of the furniture, Louis attempted to make his way into the bathroom. Staggering, he reached the bathroom. He heaved a sigh of relief upon finally stepping through the doorway, as though this was some Herculean achievement. He sighed again when he thought about his wife. He wasn't sure that she would take to his new, shall we say, outlook too well.

The electric light flickered to life. He needed it on just to confirm this new reality of his. There, staring into the mirror, he took in his strangeness. His new eye sat squarely in the middle of his forehead. There was no third eyebrow, but everything else that one would associate with a human eye was there. It blinked independently of the other two and he didn't seem capable of controlling it precisely, but otherwise, Louis thought that there was really nothing special about the eye apart from the fact that it was a late bloomer. Which is to say that he didn't discount the fact that it may have been written in his genes all along, waiting for the right moment before sprouting, before it blinked its first. Perhaps in all of us is the latent ability to see as Louis now sees. Not very well, to be frank, but surely it was just a matter of getting used to it.

Besides, who among us wouldn't be envious of having an eye to spare?

There is something miraculous about the way that most children develop into adults following some invisible Goldilocks rule—not too much and not too little. But there is always the possibility that most of us have simply failed to live up to our potential.

As we consider this rather exciting prospect heralding a new era for humanity, however, Louis was simply thinking, *I can't go to work like that.* In his mind, he could hear the dissenting voices already: "Is that your excuse? You're not going to work just because you've got three eyes? Look at Boris over there. He's only got two and he's not complaining."

Louis's thoughts went wild, and soon he feared for his job. Anxiety is a corrosive monster that too easily dissolves the struts that prop up human lives. His face became distorted, shifting into a flurry of dramatic shapes. He couldn't help fixating on how he had been away from work too much. Just two weeks ago, he was away from work for four days (six including the weekend) because of a stomach bug. The week before that, his son fell really ill, and Louis spent a day at the hospital and two at home. In short, his leave record was hardly fantastic and it worried him that his superiors would soon have an excuse, no, a reason to fire him.

"I don't want to get fired," Louis said to himself. Then he said it to himself again. It's not that he loved his job. If nothing else, it was menial and tiring, at times unbearable, but the simple truth was that it was all that he had. He had to have some way of supporting his family, paying his mortgage, and buying the occasional treat for himself. (He was particularly fond of the movies.) But there was also an existential dread that lurked beneath. If he were to lose his job, he couldn't imagine what he would spend all his time doing.

Louis continued staring at the mirror. His image was still, but his heart was pounding. Panic rose rapidly in his veins. He thought about everything he knew about third eyes, including its significance in mythologies, and its association with the spiritual. The Chinese God Erlang, for instance, uses his third eye to perceive the truth (he came across this once when he was obsessed with *Journey to the West*). Louis tried at first to comfort himself using that knowledge, but it didn't work. He knew that he did not, and would never, have such abilities. He wasn't even sure that he wanted any abilities in the first place. (God forbid that he saw any ghosts!)

All he could think about was that he had a third eye, and something was desperately wrong. It's true that he felt vaguely mythological, but only in the sense that he felt monstrous. Mythology, after all, is the realm of monsters.

So there he was, some creature in the bathroom, uncertain of his next move. Having already spent so much time in front of the mirror, he knew it wouldn't be long before his wife would come up to check on him. Furthermore, whether or not his job was at risk, there was no way he was going to show up at the office with a third eye. There was no avoiding it. He was going to have to ring the office. He decided to call his best friend at work, if they could even be called friends. Come to think of it, Louis didn't have many friends. There was this person that he was ringing, and also this other guy who sat at the other end of the office. They didn't chat a lot, had lunch together very rarely, and maybe they weren't all that close. Nevertheless, the two of them would share a good joke between them from time to time, and in this day and age, that probably counted as a friendship. Louis was bad at making friends. Or maybe he just hadn't met the right crowd. Things take time in life, such as one's career, like wisdom, like puberty, and like living and dying. Maybe his social circle was just waiting for the right time to expand. You never know. Just last night, Louis was still blinking with only two eyes. Look at him now.

When he heard a voice at the other end of the line, his eyes brightened.

"Hi," the voice said. He was mildly disappointed to learn that it was just Sue. They didn't really get along.

"I'm sorry," Louis said. "Something has happened in the house and I think I won't be coming down today. Can you help me inform the boss? I hope he doesn't throw a fit."

"I'll let him know," she promised. Her voice sounded unusually cold over the phone. "I'm sure he'll understand."

"Don't worry about it, thank you." Louis put down the receiver, biting his lower lip. He didn't share her confidence, but there was little that he could do. It had probably gone as well as it could have, but he was still unnerved by the fact that he didn't know how his superiors would react. There was every chance that he would lose his job. He felt like an incomplete sentence waiting for its missing words, waiting for actual meaning.

Nevertheless, he knew that there was no time to lose. He had to make his way downstairs before his wife grew suspicious. Louis threw on some clothes and grabbed his suitcase. He also put on a hat, intending to conceal the obscene growth. Gingerly, he attempted to creep down the stairs. He felt like a thief in his own house. With a hat on his head, sweat beading on his face, and every muscle straining to protect the silence, he felt completely ridiculous. He simply wanted to avoid a situation in which his wife came over to greet him—minimal contact, he thought. He crept quickly to the door and hid around the corner where his wife was unlikely to see him.

Quietly, he peered around the corner and looked at his son. Louis II was on all fours, clambering around the room, throwing his toys about gleefully, like some kind of cruel monster or some kind of tyrant king. Nevertheless, Louis couldn't help thinking about how much he loved his son. And his wife too. She hadn't noticed him yet. It was time to bid her a quick goodbye.

"I'll be heading out now!" he exclaimed from behind the wall.

"Louis, wait, aren't you having breakfast?"

"In a hurry!" he cried.

"But—"

"Bye!" he interrupted her. And then he went flying out the door.

He kept both his hat and his head down, taking care not to draw attention to himself. It was summer, but there was a chill in the streets that morning, and he walked briskly down slippery sidewalks. Soon enough, he found himself at the doorstep of the nearest clinic. Registration was slow, too slow, and Louis grew increasingly nervous that he would be found out before too long. He glanced around at the waiting area. It was a busy day at the clinic. One or two of the faces looked up at him. His heart skipped a few beats.

Finally, the nurse completed his registration and gave him his queue number. He snatched it from her and picked one of the few remaining empty seats. Sitting next to him was a woman with a baby a bit younger than Louis's son. The child, dressed in a pink costume, quickly took notice of the man with the hat, and couldn't resist giggling. Already nervous, this only frighted Louis, who became quite wary of the toddler. The look of mischief on his face, her face, their face—what did it matter?—said it all. Their gazes met and Louis had the awful feeling that something dreadful was going to happen. Sure enough, the child began tugging at his hat. Louis struggled to keep his disguise intact, but he also didn't want to injure the little monster. He wasn't sure if he would, but he didn't want to take any chances. Young children are sometimes extremely delicate, and sometimes extremely robust. This one was also rather feisty. Moreover, Louis had no intention of causing a commotion. So there, in the confines of that small clinic, it was monster against monster. Louis didn't know what to do. He didn't expect to find himself at the mercy of a toddler, some ten or eleven months old. All he wanted to do was to see the doctor. What further humiliation would he be subject to before he would be allowed to do so? Furthermore, his restraint meant that the child was winning. It was pure agony, his expression exclaiming, *Unhand me, child!* He made no actual noise, of course. He didn't want to be rude.

And then it happened. The child won. Louis lost his hat. He had never felt more naked in his life. An audible gasp escaped from his lips. He looked around in panic, afraid that someone would notice. To his relief, most people were half-asleep. The baby, however, was staring merrily at his abnormal face, no judgement, no disgust. Momentarily, Louis was amazed at the precious naivety of children, and he realized then that for them, reality had no set boundaries—tenuous, rich in potential, and free. With time came understanding, and with understanding came definition, until everything became limited and rigorous, until everything came under the force of law. Just then, the toddler let out a squeal of delight and Louis got a fright. He pulled his hat back from the child and replaced it just as the mother turned to look. She didn't know what had happened but gave him a dirty look just for good measure. Louis was embarrassed but relieved. His secret was safe with the child. He gave them a wink, which elicited another squeal.

Nothing of incident happened for the next half an hour, and Louis spent it fighting sleep. When his queue number was finally called, he went into the consultation room hurriedly. The doctor was a man in his forties with oily black hair and a slightly ratty face. With a voice resembling the wheeze from a deflating balloon, he went through all the formalities: *Hello. How are you? What can I do for you today?* Happy to finally be able to confide in someone, Louis sat down and quickly explained his situation. Not that it needed much explanation, mind you. He really just had to take off his hat. The look on the doctor's face betrayed no shock, no surprise. After a few more questions, the doctor seemed ready to make his diagnosis.

"Nothing to worry about," he said. "In fact, this condition is actually quite common."

"Really, doctor?" His eyes lit up in surprise.

"No, I was just joking," the doctor said. "Of course this isn't common. But I don't think it's going to be a problem. Are you in any discomfort?"

"Well, no, but—"

"That's good, then. And you can see fine now?"

"Yes, kind of, but—"

"That's good too. Any other symptoms? Nausea, maybe?"

"No. Not now. There was a little dizziness at the beginning."

"Loss of balance?"

"No."

"X-ray vision? Uhm. Just kidding! Maybe come back in a week and we'll have a look at it again. It'll probably go away."

One could hear Louis's disbelief in the silence, and then he said, "Do you have something that can help me . . . hide the condition for the time being?"

"Oh don't be silly. No one's going to notice," the doctor assured him.

"Are you sure? It's kind of . . . obvious?"

"Look, what did I say when you came in?"

"Uhm, what can I do for you today?"

"Exactly. I didn't even notice, and I'm a trained professional."

Louis looked up at the doctor's intimidating wall of certificates and plaques and for a moment—fleeting but definite—he felt that he could tell himself that the doctor was right.

Just then, the doctor surprised him by shining a bright light at the new eye. "Sorry," he apologized. "Just thought that I should be thorough."

Louis could feel his third eye reacting, and it wasn't at all comfortable. At first, he kept really quiet and even tried to smile. After all, Louis didn't want to come across as some kind of wimp. Very soon, however, he felt a bit nauseous and made his discomfort plain with a disgruntled expression. The doctor didn't notice. He strained his face harder to try to catch his attention. Nothing. And the feeling was getting more intense too. It reminded him of the nausea that he sometimes experienced during the daily commute to work. Eventually, Louis realized that he would throw up if the doctor didn't stop. Thus, he made a noise. It was then that the doctor finally noticed.

Smiling, the doctor said, "Now, now, it'll be over soon. Be good."

And Louis was good. He didn't appreciate being treated like a child, but he just wanted this to be over. Finally, after what was too long, the doctor completed his examination of the problem eye.

"I think you'll be perfectly okay. Come back next week and we'll have another look, but just for good measure, why not just take the day off from work since you're so concerned? I'll get the nurse to prepare the doctor's certificate. On the house."

Louis thought that he would take what he could get, as he knew that he would soon be paying through his nose for the consultation. The clinic was famous for having exorbitant fees, but the next nearest one was twenty-five minutes away. He sighed just thinking about all the money that he could no longer contribute to his mortgage. At least the doctor wasn't suggesting an expensive operation.

In conclusion, the doctor said, "Take some time off, get some rest, and we'll wait and see. Ha, see what I did there? Wait and *see*? For all you know, it could all be over in the blink of an eye! I'm really on a roll here."

Louis looked nonplussed. He didn't say a word as he left the consultation room, putting on his hat and slamming the door behind him. It was hard to say exactly what made him feel so uncomfortable and indignant. All he knew was that he had to get out of the place. When his name was called, he went up to the nurse and paid with some dirty bills before she could even speak. (He didn't know how much he was being charged—he simply guessed.) Bursting out from the clinic doors, he went down the street in a huff, both his pulse and his mind racing.

Feeling light-headed, he stumbled out onto the sidewalk and clumsily made his way back home. He was so confused, and he had every right to be. How was he going to go to work anymore? What would his family think? Why did this happen to him? Did it have some kind of secret meaning? The questions came torrentially, and there was only so much that Louis could take. He stopped walking and supported himself against a wall. His breathing was shallow, and the nausea was beginning to overwhelm him. He couldn't control himself as he stumbled out into the open again.

There was a dull pain in his head, as though something was slowly boring through his skull via his new eye socket. He didn't know why, but he was compelled to turn his head up and stare at the sun. The bright whiteness of the sun became a canvas on which memories, hopes, unfamiliar fears, familiar nightmares, and mirages of a life lived well were all projected. It was as if his life was blossoming before his very eyes. He tried to reach out to these images, but it was an exercise in futility. He staggered onto the concrete with tears in his eyes. The sad heap of a man trembled, and the world went dark. Then the buildings heaved, and the roads quivered, and it was as though the city was threatening to collapse on him. He knew it was a hallucination. He folded his arms and stayed still, waiting for it to pass. When he felt it was safe to move again, he scrambled to the side of the pavement and stayed crouched there. No one paid him any attention. He watched as the shoes shuffled across in front of him.

It was several minutes before he stood up again. He glanced around and was happy to see that the world had been restored. For once, its suffocating normality agreed with him.

Thus, Louis went home. When he arrived at his doorstep, he stood still and stared at its wooden frame for a long time. Checking his watch again, he tried to come up with an excuse for having returned from work so early. A breeze made him shiver slightly. He sighed. Turning the key, he opened the door, still wondering what excuse he would give his wife. It therefore caught him by surprise when he heard her shouting from the living room.

"Louis!" she cried. He was alarmed. Had she finally noticed the growth on his forehead? No, he wasn't in her line of sight. Perhaps she was going to reprimand him? They had been under some financial stress lately, with the baby and all. Surely, she didn't appreciate that he was absent from work again.

"Louis!" she cried again. Frightened, he pressed himself against the wall and peered around the corner as he did in the morning. Louis gasped, quite unable to believe the miraculous sight before his triplet eyes. He felt a mixture of elation and fear. He blinked several times in disbelief, but there was no mistaking it.

"Louis!" she cried a third time. "Louis, your son is finally walking!"

Family Dinner

Does it really matter that much that you can't remember how you got here or who these people in front of you are? It is nighttime in a boring old HDB flat, and you are seated at the table with dinner in front of you. There is a woman sitting across from you and next to her are two children. You recognize this: If you had sketched the phrase "family dinner", in your mind, it would look something like this. It's familiar, archetypal, almost a trope, and the sameness is reassuring. At least you know that you are safe. There has so far been nothing to suggest that these people mean you any harm. So, as you begin to acclimatize to the normalcy of this situation, the paranoia starts to thin, and for a moment too fleeting you imagine that you can relax. But as you adjust your chair and clear your throat, you feel the fear creeping into you again. You wonder what it is that scares you. You think that perhaps what truly frightens you is not your current reality, not what's presently staring you in the face, but that you cannot remember anything else at all; which is to say, that effectively, you've lost all of your yesterdays. Or perhaps you had no yesterdays. The space of this flat is your entire world. Perhaps you could get used to it. Aren't we always encouraged to live in the moment, to embrace the present? Nonetheless, as you try to work it out in your head, you cannot help but feel that implicit in the fact that since you have been robbed of your yesterdays, you have also been robbed of all your tomorrows. But now is not the time for existential questions. No, now is the time of danger. It is unnerving that you still don't know who these people are or how you got here. Is this woman your wife? Your sister? And how did you incur these two additional responsibilities? Why does the rice taste a little off? As these doubts and questions play across your thoughts, you know that there is nothing to guarantee that the food is not poisoned, that the children are not conspiring against you, nor that the woman won't stab you with a kitchen knife. There's no choice. You must wait for them to make their move or their mistakes. Then you'll know. For now, take care not to blow your cover. Feign ignorance as if your life depended on it. So, when the woman looks up from her plate, smiling, and asks you, "Is something wrong?" you can just look her in the eye and say, "Never been better."

Minor Illusions

One

Darryl spent the afternoon of 23 December, 2015 at the hospital. With the litany of minor ailments he had suffered in the past year, seeing the doctor was an experience that had become all too familiar. He had never, however, been to this hospital before, though he had chosen it from the appropriate list provided by his medical insurance. Of course, the word "chosen" is somewhat erroneous. He wasn't here by choice. He had an ongoing headache that no pill seemed capable of curing, and no one seemed capable of explaining, but that was the least of his worries. More frighteningly, every so often, people's faces would start to disappear. His colleagues, his parents on Skype, Brad Pitt—everyone was fair game. It was alarming even if it happened infrequently. He didn't know how he would explain it to the doctor.

The doctor was a young man who wore a massive beard, to the point that that was all there was to his face. He had a messy crop of hair, wore a plain black shirt beneath his coat, and tapped his feet rather impatiently.

"Hi, how can I help you today?" he greeted his patient, a little too loudly, a little too enthusiastically.

Darryl sat down on the chair and looked around the room, as if looking for the right words. The lights seemed just a little too bright. Perhaps afraid that the world would change the moment that he spoke, he took in as many details as he could. He couldn't help noticing the dust that had gathered on the cabinet in the corner of the room. He tried to memorize the geometry of the spinal column model that sat at the far end of the desk. Then he gathered his courage and spoke, "I've got a big migraine that's been going on for a few days now. It never subsides. It just keeps going."

"That sounds bad." There was a tone of nonchalance in his voice. "I'll give you some pills." The doctor started writing down the prescription in a terrific cursive.

Darryl felt that it was a case of speaking up or having to forever keep his peace.

"Wait, there's also this thing about faces."

"Faces?"

The pen stopped. The doctor stopped and looked up. "Tell me more," he said.

"Well, it's just, I don't know, I guess, I've been tired and this headache hasn't been helping, but I just . . . "

"Just give it to me straight."

"Yeah. It's uh, how do I put it . . . Sometimes, the faces disappear."

"Disappear?"

"Yes. I'm not sure how to put it, and I'm sure this sounds ridiculous."

"Just last week I had a patient who had a third eye growing on his forehead."

"Are you serious?"

"I might be."

There was a long pause. There was a stern frown on the doctor's face.

"Okay, well, that's my condition," Darryl said eventually. "I'm sorry I can't seem to describe it any better."

"That's okay. You're sure they disappear? You can't see the eyes or the nose or the mouth? In some cases, people lose the ability to tell faces apart, or to understand faces."

"No, I don't think it's that. They just . . . disappear completely."

"What do you see in their place then?"

"Like . . . skin?"

"Skin."

"Yes. And, it's, I don't know."

"Go on."

"Sometimes . . . Sometimes it seems like there's something moving underneath the skin. And at first I thought these were random, but I started paying attention to it more and . . . I don't know how to say this, but it's like something's trying to get out."

"That can't be good."

"No, it's not. And then there was this one time when I was in a café, right?"

"Right."

"And the thing happened and I looked across the place, and there was just this one guy who was putting his cup of coffee down, and I realised there was no face there on his head, just a head of hair and a bag of skin. I normally try to look away but then this time, something made me look closer, and I didn't want to stare, but I noticed that underneath the skin, there were four large bumps, right down the middle of his face. Like bone growths or something."

The doctor's eyes widened.

"It's okay, doctor. I'm sure I sound deranged. It's just that it started happening a bit more frequently, and so randomly that I got concerned. I'm sure it's just that I'm tired."

"No, it's not that, it's just that I feel like I should know what this is . . . "

And then, there was a flash of inspiration in his eyes.

"Give me a minute," he said. He left the desk and returned with a box of printed cards slightly smaller than photographs. Then he said, "I'm going to show you these cards and you're going to tell me what you think is printed on them, okay?"

"Like a psychiatric test."

"Yeah, just like that. Okay, this first one."

Darryl studied the card. "Looks like a deer."

"Close enough. How about this one?"

"A tree?"

"Keep going," the doctor said as he switched cards again.

"A star."

"Mmhmm."

"I think that's an owl."

"And this?"

"A semicolon."

"And this?"

"A . . . dinosaur?"

"This?"

"Fish."

"This?"

"Nothing."

"What?"

"I see nothing. The card is blank."

The doctor's face turned grim. He took out another card.

"A couple of wavy lines."

"This one?"

"A bunch of wavy lines."

"This?"

"Scribble. Looks like a cabbage."

"This one?"

"Blank."

"Okay."

"Wait, it's not blank. There are lines on it. It's like wrinkled skin."

"Wrinkled skin?"

"Yeah, like crow's feet, or palm lines."

"Okay."

"Okay."

"Well, then I think I know what the problem is with you."

The atmosphere was tense.

"It's called Metzger's Disease, named after the first person who contracted it, a certain Ulf Metzger from Germany. Its main symptom is the occasional disappearance of human faces, which occurs with increasing frequency. These faces are typically substituted."

"Substituted?"

"Like, they become replaced with something else, something unexpected. There's one report where it was just words in place of faces, and another where it was swirls and spirals. I think the worst one I read was mouths and teeth. I think that was Metzger's actually."

Darryl shuddered.

"In some cases, there are intense migraines. Sometimes patients report dryness of the eyes and persistent itches. Rarely, the tongue turns a pale yellow-green. We understand it as a neurological problem, though a physiopathology has never been identified."

"Okay, what do we do about it?"

The doctor suddenly turned and stared quite grimly at him.

"I'm sorry to have to tell you this, but there's no cure. And even worse, every recorded case of the illness—all forty-four of them—have died within two years of diagnosis. On the bright side, it means you won't incur any medical costs."

There was something about the casual manner in which he announced his verdict that seemed to soften the blow.

"I'd say we should run tests, just to be sure, but the truth is, I'm a pretty good doctor, so there's no need. I'll save you the trouble and the cash."

"I'll take your word for it," Darryl said.

"It's your life."

A long pause.

"You're sure? I'm going to die?"

"Hey, it's gonna happen to all of us someday."

"Thanks."

"My pleasure."

"What do I do?" he asked, even if he didn't honestly expect an answer.

The doctor seemed to give the question earnest thought. "You know, Metzger kept a diary. Perhaps you should too. And anyway, Metzger's diary makes for good reading. Give me another minute." The doctor rose from his chair and left the room. He came back with a book. "Look, here's a copy, fully translated."

Darryl looked at the cover. It was called *The Empty Chair*, translated by one Arno Kaufmann. He took the crummy paperback. It felt like it had passed through many hands. The pages were almost brown. Some were even flaky.

"I've never heard of this before," he said.

"Well, wasn't exactly a bestseller back in the day. It's not even that well-known among doctors because cases are so rare, you know what I mean?"

"Yeah. Okay. Thanks. Is there anything else I should expect?"

"Nothing more than I've already told."

"Will I become physically weaker? Will I need any special care?"

"Probably not. At least not from any recorded cases. It seems most of the toil and labour is emotional and mental. And death happens suddenly but peacefully if that's any consolation."

It wasn't.

"Thank you, doctor."

"My pleasure, Anyway, I was just thinking, this condition is rare, and it might present us with an opportunity. I was wondering if you'd be willing to be a part of a research project looking into Metzger's Disease. Probably won't help us identify a cure, but, you know, baby steps."

Darryl started to give it some thought.

"I mean, hey, if you don't want to do it, I can understand. I know you've more important things to think about right now."

Darryl stopped giving it any thought. "Well, if you put it that way."

"Too bad, then," the doctor said. "In any case, I'm afraid that's all I'm going to be able to do for you today. Do come back if you've got any questions, develop any uncomfortable symptoms, or need any letters or the like."

Darryl nodded. He took a deep breath before rising from the chair. Everything that followed felt all too by-the-numbers. He waited for his number and name to be called again. He flashed his insurance card at the counter, smiled as best he could, paid the difference, mumbled a thank you. He kept the receipt in his back pocket. Then he walked down the long corridor, past the waiting area, past the vending machine, past the faulty light. Echoes. Voices. Machinery. The sound of his shoes landing on the floor.

The automated doors coldly slid open, and he stood pausing at the fringe between the sterile hospital interiors and the noise-filled, sun-baked world outside. He could hear the wind whistle in the distance. He rubbed his hands together and took another deep breath before stepping into the sun, the bright, blue earth, the chaos-world. Shielding his eyes from the sun's glare as he emerged, he suddenly felt old, tired. He had come out of the doors expecting the world to feel different, expecting it to look bleaker, sadder, or perhaps more beautiful, but nothing had really changed. The sun felt more distant then, if anything—as if it wasn't already distant enough. He checked his phone for the time and thought about what to do with the rest of the day, and indeed, what to do with the rest of his life. He felt no anger, no anguish, and hardly any despair. Maybe it wasn't time yet. Above him, the square-shaped sky seemed to take on the mantle of a god. Uncertain of what to do, he rang up the office and took the day off.

Two

Darryl worked for a small software company from Singapore with a new office on the West Coast. He had applied to the Singapore main office, but was assigned to the American branch as soon as he accepted the job offer to help get it off the ground. From a young age, he aspired to be a writer but soon realized that nothing about that dream was realistic. Uncertain about what to do, he applied to a wide variety of jobs. This was one of the three that got back to him, and he first interviewed for it about a year and a half before. It went well enough, and soon he was called back for a second interview. The third interview took place some four weeks after. The company was housed in an immense building of metal and glass. At the lobby, he traded his credentials for a visitor's pass and took the lift up twenty-two floors. An HR officer let him in through the glass doors, and he sat waiting for about half an hour. It seemed to be going swimmingly until one of the directors broke his silence and began to interrogate him. Questions that he had to answer included: *Why would the university allow you to take a degree in literature after your engineering degree? If you were so interested in working in the tech industry, why did you work as a research assistant in the university for two years?* He didn't understand. He didn't know what the questions were intended for and was suspicious of their unusual reductive quality. He felt out of the loop, uncertain of what was expected of him, as though the questions were manipulating him into making some kind of nasty confession. How much of one's life story is appropriate at a job interview? Was it fair for him to comment on things that he didn't know? He just did his best.

It was four weeks before he heard from the company again, and the news surprised him. The voice on the other side said that they were making him an offer.

"Great," he said.

"However, we want you to join our new office overseas."

"That sounds exciting," Darryl said with as much sincerity as he could muster.

"Good. We feel that we want you to help in getting it off the ground."

And that was how he ended up in America. The first three months were mostly training, learning the ropes, setting things up. His girlfriend Rebecca, a postgrad student at Berkeley, popped by for a few days to help with the process. Rent was startlingly high, and he bunked in with a Turkish programmer who worked for IBM and appeared to be very good at his job. Darryl did not spend too much time with his roommate. They conversed each day very briefly. Things were amicable but it did seem as though the two housemates were not all that interested in each other. Darryl came home every evening and stayed mostly in his room with the lights off, watching videos on YouTube or playing video games.

Every morning, he arrived at work feeling far more tired than he believed he should. Initially, he believed it to be a problem with the jet lag, but it persisted for so long that he decided it was some type of strange affliction. In retrospect, perhaps it was simply an unidentified symptom of Metzger's Disease.

He always took a bus to work because he didn't know how to ride a bicycle, and he was in no hurry to learn because he found it useful to catch up on sleep during the bus ride. Sure, it was embarrassing because sometimes his head would begin lolling all over like some kind of drunken snake, and he never knew when he would wake up resting on the shoulders of some too-friendly commuter, but he felt like it was crucial to his morning routine. Soon, he realized, of course, that none of this sleep helped. If anything, it only seemed to make him feel even more fatigued. Yet, by then, it was so deeply embedded into his everyday routine that he could no longer imagine life without it.

It didn't seem reasonable to believe that his colleagues were suffering from the same affliction. Appearances could be deceiving, but as far as he could tell, they were able to get on with their work just fine. No, in fact, they were doing much more than just fine. He heard these stories about his colleagues partying till daybreak, or pulling all-nighters in the hopes of promotions, but they still looked alert and attentive. They also always seemed to be busy with something. It was certainly possible that he was merely paranoid and that their different positions meant that they had different assignments—ones that didn't wear them out in the same way—but he couldn't help speculating. Using a variety of strategies—regular bathroom breaks, frequent hydration, stretching exercises, standing desk—he did his best to stay alert enough to avoid damaging office morale.

There he sat in his cubicle, managing to stay awake but unable to fend off the yawning. The sounds of keyboards around him formed some unintentional chorus. He imagined his head bobbing along to the monotonous rhythm. He strained his ears and tried to listen to the office chatter, hoping that some juicy story would tickle him awake.

It baffled him. He didn't sleep all that late. He had what he imagined was a normal diet. He rarely consumed alcohol (he couldn't afford that lifestyle), and he had no caffeine addiction, so it seemed safe to eliminate beverages as the main cause of his fatigue problems. He theorized that there was something bio-logically wrong with him, not quite chronic fatigue syndrome, but chronic enough and fatigue enough. Perhaps, he thought, it was the quality of his sleep that was a problem. He once saw on television something about the importance of sleep health and the need to consult the right doctors. Unfortunately, there were no specifics that he could quite recall from the segment.

He looked around again, studying the straight lines, the rectangular shapes, the sameness of the textures. There was something charming about how dull the office was. He thought about how each morning he woke up from his dreams only to be returned to the everyday, the normal. Every so often, he found the blandness of everyday life terrifying. It was unmappable and unreadable. Indigestible. Its blandness was stifling. He thought of how it was impossible to recognize every change in the everyday landscape, and perhaps its constant change, the everyday managed to simulate stillness. There was a quality of facelessness to everyday life. It had no face. Perhaps that was what was so unbearable about working in the office.

Sometimes it would terrify him—the notion of the everyday. He imagined himself, lost in this sea of sameness, unable to define himself and his self. True, he had often read, heard, and seen stories about people with the most mundane lives, but in stories, their numbness or nausea seemed magnified. They were tropes. They were convenient storytelling devices. He understood them as projections. As he stood up in the office, looking around, studying the sameness, the mundanity or banality that surrounded him, he understood not just its intensity, but also its magnitude. He despaired at the thought that the everyday belonged to him, or perhaps that he belonged to the everyday. It was an infection.

Three

In the days following the first diagnosis, Darryl sought a second opinion, and then a third, a fourth, a fifth. (It was no minor fall, but he could use a major lift.) The first diagnosis soon became the only diagnosis. He had this obscure and lethal disease and there was nothing he could do to change it. Reality only solidified with every consultation.

He also spent a lot of time on the internet, attempting to find out more about his condition. Indeed, the internet was his only companion. The spectre of a terminal disease had robbed him of his ability to socialize. Having decided to keep his troubles to himself for the time, he discovered that he could not engage in any conversation with a reasonable degree of sincerity while protecting his secret. They took on the texture of artificiality. He could no longer take ownership of his words. Instead of feeling that he was wearing a mask, he felt that he *was* the mask.

At the time, he had yet to shake the feeling that it was all some kind of a prank, or worse, that he was just a part of some reality television show. He found precious little online, apart from the occasional, no-longer-maintained GeoCities website or LiveJournal post. The Wikipedia entry was terse and uninformative. He also tried looking up books. Apart from Metzger's diary, he also came across *The Faceless Brain* by Karen

Kassel. The blurb made it sound like a novel, but he placed an order for it anyway. There was also a Dutch book that went for an exorbitant amount on a rare books website. He didn't read Dutch but placed an order for it just in case. At the same time, he worked on more generic research, reading more generally about the neuroscience behind face recognition. He spent night after night in this way, trawling through the internet, certain that he would discover something new.

He had a lot of trouble sleeping, anyway. It wasn't the same as his perpetual fatigue at the workplace either. Beginning from the day of his diagnosis, he went to bed late and found himself awake far too early. His rest was restless. He dreamt often, and of wildly different things. He could also remember his dreams quite well. One time, he dreamt that he was a cloud that didn't know what shape to take, whether camel, weasel, or whale. It seemed that he was unaware that he possessed the shape of a cloud. Another time, he dreamt that he was a mirror, a fragile coincidence of the object and the subject, a signifier trying to become a sign, able to hold every image except its own. Often, he dreamt that he was a shadow in search of his own shadow. Twice now, he dreamt that he was his friend Joyce. Once, he dreamt that he was some creature from Japanese folklore, some type of ancient spirit whose wits got the better of himself. He was on the verge of dying, or at least some form of terrible suffering, and on the cusp of his death, he questioned the nature of his consciousness. Perhaps he was an individual making his own choices, suffering his own karmic retribution, or perhaps he was merely a sign living up to some imaginative mythology, fulfilling some destiny.

Four

One morning, Darryl decided to quit his job. He started the day with great trepidation, as he was sure that his superiors wouldn't make such a sudden resignation easy. Besides, would anyone really believe that a disease like Metzger's existed? Still, a deep yearning for home developed in the aftermath of the diagnosis—he had to return to Singapore.

When he entered her office, his manager was looking distractedly at a computer screen.

"How can I help you?" she said.

"Well, uh, I'm leaving the job."

"I'm sorry?"

"It's, uh, it's a long story. I got diagnosed with this terminal disease—actually, I don't know if I can even call it that—a few days ago, and I've been sitting on the news unsure of what to do since. I mean, it's not exactly a common disease, but—"

"Are you okay?" she asked. She looked up at him, stared at his face, studying it for any sign that it was a joke.

"Yup. It's just . . . It's terminal."

"What are you down with?"

"It's, uh, it's called Metzger's Disease."

"Oh. I think I had an uncle who had it."

"Oh."

They spent a long while in silence. When Darryl looked up at her again, he noticed that her face had gone. It was happening again. He tried not to stare, but he noticed that this time, there was something different. There was something advancing down the sides of her head, like a rigid sheet, the color of pearl, slowly covering her skin fully like a shard of carapace.

"Hey, are you okay?" she asked again.

He snapped out of it. "Uh, yeah. Sure. I am."

"Look, I know it's a lot to deal with. Take all the time you need."

He nodded. "I figured if I'm going to die, I should do it back home."

"That . . . that makes a lot of sense," she said. She sighed. And then, she offered him her sympathies and suggested a helpful arrangement for his resignation with a generous amount of compassionate leave. He could take his time vacating the office, the leave would help with any visa issues, and he could still get paid for a bit more. He just nodded through the conversation. When they agreed on the course of action, he thanked her earnestly as she rang up HR. It almost seemed to go too smoothly. He was grateful, but he was struggling with her facelessness. The uncanniness of a voice emerging from no mouth was never going to get easier to deal with, but in that moment, there was a question he couldn't get out of his mind.

What are these faces transforming into?

She told him that he could go for the day, and that while he could take his time vacating his position and handing off his work, he didn't really have to come back if he didn't want to. He went back to his desk and realized that he didn't have much that he had to pack. He sat for a while at his desk and decided to let Rebecca know all that had happened.

"Hi, Rebecca," he said.

"What's up? You sound . . . strange."

"I, uh— Is it a convenient time?"

"I guess so."

He took in a deep breath. "I've already left my job, and I don't have long to live."

"Excuse me?"

"I'm sorry. I know this seems like the worst excuse for a break-up. I'm totally a shit person. I'm heading back home in a month or so. I just . . . I didn't want to be a burden."

"What's it called?"

"What?"

"The disease."

"Metzger's."

"Metzger's Disease? I think I've heard of it."

"What? Seriously?"

"Yeah. Is it the one about the faces?"

"Yes."

"I've heard of it."

"Okay."

There was a long silence between them. Darryl found it funny that in all of this he had been the only person who had any trouble accepting the existence of Metzger's Disease.

After a moment's pause, she continued and said, "My semester's almost over. Why don't I come over once I'm done and we can go to Singapore together? Just give me a couple more weeks." Darryl agreed. He had no words. He couldn't say anything else for the rest of the phone call.

After that, he went off. He waved to the security officer at the lobby, but he didn't wave back. He was a true professional. Darryl went to the large glass doors and pushed them open. They opened like the airlock of a space shuttle. In front of it, the world, the vast world, the wail and the heat and the salt of the earth. Somehow, the bustle of the city scared him. The world looked distorted, like it had been through the curvature of a lens. He took a moment, before stepping out into the waning sunlight. He felt as if he could watch himself walking out of the doors, as if through a television. He wasn't sure where that faintly voyeuristic feeling came from. There was a sense of displacement, as if he had rehearsed this moment so many times that the only thing left to do was to watch. Before long, he found himself fading, cut up, atomized, reconstructed, making his way into the pall and pallor, the dust and darkness. Before long, he found himself in the noise, in the chaos, in the familiar embrace of the tyrant sea.

Five

That night, without a destination in mind, Darryl took a bus out somewhere. He didn't know what bus it was. He just boarded it, paid the fare, and took a seat in the back. When the scenery outside was satisfactorily nondescript, he got off the bus. There was only one other passenger on it, fast asleep, as he watched the bus speed away.

There were houses around. It wasn't completely deserted. He walked down the hill and navigated his way through this small residential area, feeling like he was making his way through the set of *The Goonies*. He checked the GPS on his phone. It didn't seem like such a long walk. He'd be on the edge of the city in forty-five minutes or so, if Google Maps was to be believed. But before too long, the houses gave way to trees, and the streetlights cast shadows. He must have taken a wrong turn somewhere and had somehow ended up in the woods. He kept walking. In the distance, he could see electric lights. He checked the map and confirmed that he was headed in the right general direction. There was the sound of running water, maybe a stream, maybe a drain, but he couldn't see it. The darkness was suffocating. The lights looked further than he remembered, as though they were slowly being snuffed out. He could feel danger in the air. Perhaps it was a natural reaction to the darkness. He didn't think he had the good luck of being preyed on by lurking criminals—why would they even be out here?—but he wasn't privy to their methods. He had flashes of *Twin Peaks* and wondered if his body would be discovered along the riverbank the next day. He chuckled nervously. How could someone who had already made peace with his death be afraid of dying? What, then, was he afraid of?

He started walking faster, and then, when he could bear it no longer, he began to run. He knew that it was dangerous to run ahead because he was unable to see beyond the light that came from his phone, but he didn't stop. It was instinctive, impulsive. He wanted out of the abyss.

Eventually, when his breathing gave him too much trouble, he slowed down. His sense of urgency, however, had not dimmed. He heard the ring of a bell, and saw the flashing strobe of a bicycle's light, and turned back. He felt some kind of hope that that the shroud could be pierced. "To your left," he heard. Darryl hopped to his right instinctively. He felt the cyclist going past, nothing more than wind and echo. Then cyclist was gone, if he was ever there. "Just an illusion," he whispered to himself under his breath. Nothing could enter or leave the darkness. It was hermetic, which is to say that there was no knowing what was even possible. He realized then that without his observing the world, his reality had contracted. The limits of his observation were the shape of his world. He could not see beyond the darkness, but his memories were also fast fading. His connection to the world seemingly severed, he was no longer sure of its existence, no longer sure that anything else existed. And yet, without anyone else to see him, to authenticate him, he understood that he too must have been unsubstantiated, receding quickly into non-existence. He could feel his own memory and knowledge decaying, the gradually growing darkness encroaching not only into the extent of his reality but also his minute existence.

Before he realized it, the night had subsided. He felt his shoes landing on asphalt. He wasn't sure how long he had been running. He wanted to keep running, to escape somewhere; and as his feet gathered pace once again, he began to understand that there is no place that they can take him because every place is simply one place. The taste of the air was salty and familiar. In the distance, the honking of cars and the voices of the homeless. He thought he spotted shadows in the shape of pedestrians. Yet, still buoyed by some unnatural momentum, or perhaps driven by fear, he kept on running. Gradually, the city unfolded about him, crisscrossing and zigzagging. He couldn't stop. He had to keep running. He knew that there was a place for him somewhere in the night. The lights bore down on him. He could feel himself panting, but it wasn't him, just the hissing sound of a body, a husk in the shape of a man. He ran his legs off, as fast and as far as they would carry him, keen to expend all his energy. He didn't understand it. Maybe if he had given everything, what was left behind could finally be true.

The city continued to draw him in, into its hazy sprawl of lights, and its humid darkness. Lights. Glass diffusion. Kaleidoscope colours. Everything looked like nothing in the quicksilver night. There were streaks and blurs and hollows, and nothing he could recognize. He couldn't tell if he was going in the right direction. Impossible to differentiate one place, one corner, one turn, from another, another, another. Impossible to tell to where or from what he was running. Reality became slippery and amorphous. He had to rearrange the shapes with his mind, hoping that somehow, they would turn out the way they used to be. He could feel himself tightly tethered to the reality around him. Any moment then, the cord could snap.

His feet now racing, his mind spiralling, he imagined cannibals, blood-letters, and body-snatchers. The lights were poison, twisting and turning, oscillating, hypnotizing, spinning perpetually, hiding some kind of unbearable truth. The lights were poison, and he had to run, but he couldn't outrun the lights. He crashed to his knees, unable to continue. He could feel the acid in his muscles. He knelt there on the cold pavement, waiting on the edge of darkness, dying for oxygen, alone, motionless. There was not a single sound in the night.

Somehow, he managed to stand again. He kept going, at a walking pace this time. The world around him slowed down into a recognizable sight. The streets were still dark, but he could see that he was in a residential area. Then, as he felt the oxygen gradually returning to his body, he started to see familiar buildings and streets. There was no doubt about it. He had somehow ended up in the university district. It was good news because he knew how to make his way back to his place from there. It was also a relatively safe area. He was in the right part of the neighbourhood. There was a chill in the air. He staggered down the pavement clumsily. He must have looked a little drunk to anyone who was watching.

Suddenly, a voice, "Hey, man, wanna come in for a dance?"

The sentence didn't register. He stared at the man, almost looking past him. He still had his face. He was young, had brown hair, and looked like he went to the gym regularly. Darryl breathed a sigh of relief.

"You wanna come in for a dance?" he repeated himself, posing the question like the beginning of some Faustian bargain. His face looked suspicious—too well-groomed, too overeager a smile. "You won't be dancing with me, of course," he continued. "You could be dancing with any number of girls in there." Darryl didn't like the sleazy tone of his voice, and he was also not a dancing sort, and had trouble imagining what it was like dancing with any girl or girls. That sounded like a nightmare.

"Oh come on, it'll be fun," he heard. He felt a hand on his shoulder gently tugging at him. Darryl looked at the large brick building, saw the bright lights from within, heard the voices of teenagers. He surmised that it was a frat house having some kind of a party. Were they looking for a victim? Were they just looking to fill up the house? Was it such a sad party that they had to ask an unattractive Asian guy to join in? It sounded like a huge scam. It probably was a huge scam.

He tried to move along, but the man was persistent, and Darryl was out of breath. Darryl looked up at him only to realize that it had happened. The face had vanished. In its place was creased skin, like on a pruned finger.

"Come on."

Overwhelmed by disgust, Darryl wanted to go. But there was something beckoning to him, something that wouldn't settle in his mind. He looked at the house and it was as though it was somehow expecting him, as though all the secrets to his absurd medical condition lay within its walls.

So, he didn't say no. He relented and nodded, bought the Faustian bargain. He was a little curious. He had to catch his breath. He let the fellow shepherd him in.

Darryl entered the building not knowing quite what to expect. Beginning to regret his decision, he took a seat in a corner of a room and sat there studying what was unfolding around him. The hall seemed far too busy. He saw people in different stages of inebriation. *No one will even notice that I'm here*, he thought. Someone came up to shake his clammy hand, another muscular chap who looked like he played football. He checked the faces and, as far as he could tell, they were all still there. His mind still hazy, he tried to be as courteous as possible. He needn't have worried because there was hardly anyone within who gave him a second glance. In fact, the hall inside was far too empty. It made him a little nervous. Not only because he couldn't help wondering if he had walked into some kind of trap, but also because there was no crowd that he could blend into.

He overheard a conversation:

"How have you been?"

"The same, I suppose. You?"

"The same. I suppose."

"Nice place."

"Yeah."

"Had a good semester?"

"I didn't have a bad semester. Didn't do so well for that math class, but I'll live. How did yours go?"

"Not terribly."

"Who else will be coming?"

"I don't know. But I guess the night's still young, you know?"

"Yeah. Say, I'm getting a beer. You want one?"

"Uh, no, thanks. I'll, uh, help myself later."

Darryl surmised that it was probably an end-of-semester party of some sort. He had no clue about the inner workings of fraternities and simply assumed that that was a tradition. He felt like a fraud, having been invited into proceedings essentially by mistake. He was no college student, and while the implication that he looked young enough to pass for one was strangely flattering, he felt that he had to keep the illusion alive, pretend that he was a student of some sort, or at least someone's friend. This made him especially anxious as he attempted to get a drink, to the point that he lost his nerve and just sat back down on the plastic chair, listening to plastic voices.

Someone came to greet him. It was a student from China. It turned out to be a mistake. He must have resembled a friend of his. Darryl didn't know quite how to respond, and a curious expression contorted his face. Upon discovering his mistake, the student apologized and turned to go, his embarrassment plain to see. Somehow, Darryl felt obliged to apologize too, but the student had already scurried away.

He decided to take it easy, bide his time, keep a low profile, and maybe flee when no one was looking. The walls were lined with balloons. There was a fancy table that someone had spent a lot of effort setting up and no one had spent a lot of time appreciating. The rest of the decorations looked sad. Party streamers sagged and resembled earthworms. Some balloons were already deflated. A chorus of loud hoots and whistles upstairs told him where the party was really happening. There was a lot of food, but in spite of all the running that he had done that night, he didn't feel compelled to try any of it. He took a seat on a chair after narrowly avoided stepping on a drunk person on the ground.

He looked to his left and focused on another unfolding conversation. One of the guys was a little overdressed for the occasion, a proper shirt and a striped tie, like he was trying to sell something. The other looked dressed for the beach.

"So, what are you doing now?"

"Oh, I'm, uh, I've been looking for a job."

There was some nervous laughter.

"How's it going?"

"Not too well. Times are rough. I just had an interview this afternoon for a job as a recruiter. I don't think they were all that interested."

"Well, keep trying. The job market's really bad, but you could get lucky."

"How's it going for you?"

"Not too well either. Times are rough."

"What do you think of this party?"

"I don't know, man. Could use a bit more life. Some people are already drunk. What do *you* think of this party?"

"Could use a bit more life."

"Yeah."

"Yeah."

The conversation was nondescript, but he was struck by the unusual repetition of lines. Had casual conversations been this way all along? A feeling of uncanniness arose within him. He looked up at the faces of the two oddly dressed individuals once more and found that they had changed, becoming less well-defined, more similar, equalized, anonymous.

It was happening. The faces were going. He turned away, frightened. He took in a deep breath, then several more. None of it was new, of course, but he was gripped by an awful sense that he was at some kind of tipping point. He found enough courage to look up at the two guys again, and in the dim light, he saw their faces changing, shifting. There were multiple protrusions that seemed to be coming out of the skin where their faces would have been. He wasn't sure what he was looking at, until he saw the protrusions bend, curling inwards and out. They were jointed. They were fingers.

He turned away. A tall woman at the corner of the room caught his eye. She had dark hair and her face was featureless as well. He squinted and thought that the skin was shifting with disturbing vigor. He knew it was happening. Her face was turning into fingers too.

It happened suddenly. He blinked and there they were, sprouting from her skin, fifteen or twenty digits. He couldn't look away. The fingers were uniform in size and their movements seemed coordinated. It was as if they were searching for some configuration, trying to settle into some sort of final state. Slowly, they curled around each other, interlocking in a circular shape that resembled a blooming flower.

It was all just an illusion, he told himself. All these faces were still there. He was sure of it. But he could feel things slipping away. Slowly but surely, his reality seemed to drift into erasure. Everything slowed down and seemed imbued with an unnatural weightlessness.

Closing his eyes, he thought of Rebecca, thought of her face, her hair and its patterns, the sound of her voice, scents, skin. And then, nothing. There was suddenly nothing of her that he could remember. He could remember a face, but it was only a collection of lines that didn't make sense to him. He remembered reading in Metzger's diary about the possible loss of cognition and memory. He had written: "No longer do I trust the presence of people dear to me. No longer do I trust the illusion of the world."

He stood to his feet and wanted to leave immediately. He felt ill. His existence was incongruous, incoherent, tenuous. He could not string together a single rational thought. However, he was hit immediately by a sudden spell of giddiness. His legs wobbled. He had to steady himself using the chair. There was a throbbing in his head. He could feel it swelling, saw its form becoming irregular, like a lump, a cyst, a tumour. Confusion, fear, and anger start to overtake him. He tried to calm down. He felt acid churning within his stomach. His blood was dilute. His head spinning, he saw himself sucked into a vacuum in which his shape becomes elongated and horrific. He saw his eyes stretched into parallel lines, his mouth a pout and then a scream, his figure a spindly distortion. As his imagination became taut and bent, so did his figure, his skeleton, his twisted tongue, stretched across infinite amounts of nothing, yet unable to snap.

Disquiet—an awful and insurmountable disquiet—like a toothache or a migraine that had grown with malicious intent over the course of years—now wielding his limbs as a puppet's, now twisting him as a strip of wire—now, sickness. He became a caricature of himself, damp with sweat, quivering, skittering, and shaking. He felt like vomiting, but sickeningly, he found himself unable to do so. The illness felt like a knife lodged in his abdomen. It hit him like the tides, stronger one moment, weaker the next, then stronger than before.

He saw a vision of a pill dissolving in a tall glass of water, mushrooming into a cloud of dust. The external world was stretched into a horrid curve, enshrouding him, refusing to let him out of his immaculate vertigo. His thoughts ran amok. He thought of the scales of a snake, then mountains of ice, then a face under the door, then all the names, then the lotus flowers, and then he began to think that he was only reading a story of himself in this malevolent illness.

Slowly his mouth opened into the stale and endless air, and thus, he found the strength to stand. He entered a restroom without realizing it. He was on his knees feeling dreadfully ill, a strange sickness surging from his gut. He asked for pain, and nothing but pain. Pain to overcome the sickness or at least the numbness; the pain of catharsis, the pain of excision, the pain of simple living. He staggered to his feet, supported himself against the sink, stared into his mirror, hands on his face. Gradually, his fingers seemed to push into his skin, his flesh, and he saw sinew, calcium, brain matter, as far as his fingernails could reach. Nothing was beyond his reach. He parted his flesh as a god parts the sea. Reality was fast losing meaning, could no longer contain it. Everything was sick and everything sickened him, everything sighed.

He started convulsing. He was a shadow that had lost its person, a flickering shape. He was a crumpled skeleton engaged in an electric dance. His body was reacting to something, trying to empty him of his sickness. Then he retched. The sound that came from his throat was dreadful. When it was over, he spent time studying the contents of his stomach in all its filth, looking for signs and symbols in its poisonous repetition.

There was, at least, temporary respite.

He sat on the floor with his face at the edge of the toilet bowl, feeling depressed.

He hadn't known this magnitude of powerlessness before. Perhaps it was a side effect of Metzger's Disease. Or perhaps he had simply run too hard for too long. He blinked and saw his face again in the mirror. He knew that he was looking at nothing. *I'm not here*, he observed, but felt as though the words belonged to someone else. The image of his face was fleeting. He saw an emptiness again. He also noticed a stain on his clothes. He tried to wash it off at the sink. He felt unseemly, unclean, but there was little that he could do about it.

Staggering to his feet, he tried frantically to flush the toilet. He was ashamed of his sick, and he didn't want anyone see him next to his crime. It wasn't his fault. He didn't want to be sick. It was taking a while. He was afraid that someone was going to knock on the door. After the sixth attempt, there were almost no more visible signs. Satisfied with the result, he attempted to leave the restroom. As he stepped through the door, legs still wobbling, he was abandoned by his sense of balance. His vision, too, began playing tricks on him, doubling reality and feeding it into a swirl. There was a tautness in his muscles, a pressure too well-suited to his shape. He was not so much caged as he was enveloped, encased in a silhouette tailored to his nausea.

For an instant, he believed that he heard screaming, terrible and inhuman screaming, but he knew too well that it was only the sound of the party distorted by the feelings of sickness. Maybe someone could help him.

"Hello?" he hollered down the corridor, without the hope of a response, taking refuge in the echo of his voice. Nothing. The tiled floor and expressionless walls formed a forest, a landscape informed by a sameness so much like sand. The lights were glaring, turning his skin sick and stale. His anguish bloomed. It was suffocating. Everything collapsed within the space of his mind, everything disassembled, everything deconstructed, from stories to sentences to words. He just had to breathe.

Darryl made it out into the main hall again. He could feel the illness waning. Perhaps he just needed more time. He thought better of calling for help, confident that he would make it through without stirring up any trouble. His breathing was shallow and he looked sick, but he was sure that no one paid him enough attention to notice. They probably imagined that he was drunk. As he went by a large table, he took a moment to compose himself. He picked up a lukewarm can of beer, hoping it would alleviate his condition, and snapped it open as he sat down.

Beside him, there was a woman with two hands for a face. They chatted for twenty seconds but weren't able to get anything going. He just turned away awkwardly. They sat in this state of unease for several minutes before someone approached, asking her for a dance. Darryl stared at the empty space that the stranger left behind. As he tried to recover from his sudden illness, he was left with the feeling that he was merely a vessel for an extrinsic consciousness, his eyes simply reporting back what he was seeing, his mind merely processing instructions. He had no agency, no independent thought, no possibility of knowing his extant purpose.

He watched as the party unfolded before him. The lights seemed to go dim. He knew it was only his imagination. Figures drifted into his field of view. Some of the bodies lying on the floor began to stir. A faint haze clouded his vision. It looked like a garden in which contrived angels bloomed, a theatre of mirages pretending to be human, conjuring the impression of young souls.

Darryl found it impossible to look away.

Teenagers danced to the guitar fuzz, their skeletal frames twitching like marionettes in stop-motion, as if guided by instruction or destiny. The young and faceless swayed to music, and it occurred to him that surely he too was the same. If he could look at himself, surely he too would be as faceless as the crowd. So he saw in them a mutual facelessness, dancing in the dimming light in some familiar way, manipulated by an extrinsic force, out of sight and out of mind, invisible and undetectable.

Six

Rebecca arrived on a Thursday. She'd taken a morning flight from Texas and even though the flight had been delayed, it still landed before noon. When she arrived at his door, he embraced her without a word. This wordlessness characterized the following hours as well, moments spent in a calm silence as well as some tears. The only words she said before lunch were, *You've lost weight.*

Reality proved stable and reliable for the moment. Darryl was thankful for that. He wondered if her presence calmed him, and if that had a positive effect on his condition. They had a quiet meal together at a Thai restaurant that he liked. Winter continued to be unkind, and there was a mild rain accompanied by disproportionately strong winds. They browsed shops, held hands, cracked jokes, and had coffee. Then they bought the supplies they would need for packing: a good pair of scissors, large Ziploc bags, a few boxes of varying dimensions, and several rolls of tape. He relied on her know-how, honed from years of graduate school and too-frequent moving.

They returned early in the evening. There was no one at home. They prepared a simple dinner with whatever he had in the fridge. Subsequently, they got to packing, making full use of the boxes and tape. As he packed, he pondered on what had precipitated this turn of events. He had long realized that cause-and-effect was a simple enough concept but an unpredictable master. Perhaps if he hadn't made the trip across the ocean, things would have been fine. It was hard to say.

They stopped for the evening and spent the rest of the night looking at their old photographs. They looked younger, unmistakeably themselves, yet also somewhat different, like imitators of a sort. They enjoyed making the goofiest of faces in them. He studied every expression, as if each was a marker of some lost moment, some irretrievable past, knowing too well that he was in search of something that was out of reach. He was slightly amazed at the elasticity of his own face and thought that every face had no default state, pliable and impermanent.

The next few days went by quickly. They spent each one in roughly the same manner, until one afternoon when there was no more packing to be done.

Occasionally, he would have to deal with the disappearing faces. It seemed to be happening with increasing frequency now. Hands were his theme. Sometimes, he'd spot someone with a terrifying number of fingers on their heads. Sometimes, he'd see a grasping hand in place of a face, straining to reach out into the rest of the world, like some grotesque monster on the cusp of being given life.

They spent his remaining days in America checking off the things to do on his bucket list. He finally went to the local art museum. They went for a meal at the fancy Japanese restaurant he had had his eye on for ages. They embarked on a quest to try every single gelato spot in the city. They managed to fit in a three-day visit to Seattle, where they visited sea lions, an anarchist bookstore, and a bridge troll. They took a lot of photographs during this time, supposedly making memories, but really just committing their days to the expansion of their photographic archive, becoming signs. He didn't mind. He felt certain that he would soon be unable to remember the days that they had shared, and it didn't seem so bad that those memories were somehow externalized, preserved in a domain outside of his subjective self. The semiotic nature of romance deepened.

They were merely repeating patterns, staging a romance guided by the particular shape of the world. Every photograph and every outing served only to confirm this reality, reinforce its structure. They had become signs themselves, perpetuating the norms of romance. Yet, he didn't think of it cynically, at least insofar as he understood that it was only through this illusive cycle that they could find something true.

He knew that she was trying her best to take his mind off of things, but he found himself at a loss most of the time because he didn't know how they could properly spend their last days together. He wanted to do so much in the little time he had left, but he also wanted to avoid turning their last days together into a frantic race against time. Every one of these moments felt urgent, precious, but he knew that they had to let them occur naturally, to let them breathe.

Complicating matters was the fact that he did not quite know how to deal with their relationship. There was guilt, but also a type of pity. He didn't want to be a burden to her, and he had long felt that it was enormously unfair to expect anything of her. The events of the party night disturbed him greatly, and he feared the onset of some type of dementia. He could see himself being unable to remember the most important things, and then, failing to even make sense of the world around him. Knowing all too well that it would place an unfair and unnecessary burden on her, he thought of speaking with Rebecca about it. Yet, the emotions were crude, and he never quite found a way to start.

One evening, when they had run out of things to do and places to see, he took several blank sheets of paper and a few markers. He asked, quite simply, if she would like to draw. He wasn't very good at it, but he knew that she was, and he felt that it was a thing he had wanted them to do together for a long time.

When he was a child, he sketched Spider-Man by copying frames from his comic books. He drew badly and only did it because he was convinced that Spider-Man was the best thing that had ever happened to him. He never learnt anything about composition or perspective. He didn't learn anything about shading. He wasn't even able to draw a line with a steady hand, thus producing sheet after sheet of Spider-Man sketches with inconsistent proportions and unusual musculature.

"What do we draw?" she asked. "Anything you like," he said. They sat on the floor and began drawing. Darryl doodled aimlessly: first a penguin, then a tree, and then a few abstract shapes. And then, when it was clear that it was going nowhere, he just said simply, "Teach me?" She laughed. They started with animals. Under her instruction, he spent more time visualizing what he was going to put to paper before beginning. He also paid attention to the angle of the pen and the force applied by his hand. He came up with a number of ugly but decidedly cute creatures that resembled animals known to science. They reminded him of his origami work.

"Okay, let's try something more complex. Human figures," he said. So they started to draw human figures. He had vague flashes of the way he used to draw Spider-Man when he was a kid but resisted the urge to return to old ways.

He hadn't noticed before, but he thought then that Rebecca had the talent of a cartoonist, sketching characters little and large with precise exaggeration. On the other hand, he produced indistinct shapes like bodies in motion, using just simple lines. He imagined all of his sketches being dancers mid-twirl and felt quite proud of himself.

Eventually, when they had exhausted the subject matter, he said, "Faces". His voice trembled, as though he had uttered something unspeakable. He felt that he was tempting fate. What good could possibly come out of this? "Okay," she said. "Just simple ones will do."

She started by demonstrating how she went about drawing faces. He watched carefully as she applied pen to paper. He knew what each line meant, how each marking was allocating space to a specific facial feature, but he knew that he would struggle to put it together.

"Guide me," he said when it was his turn. She took his hand and, rather clumsily, they tried to draw a face, producing several failures and some laughter. As he went on, however, he realized that the sketches were making less and less sense to him. Each face was breaking down into its lips, its nose, its eyes, and each of these, lines. Soon, it was all just a jumble in his mind. He was unable to see the big picture, so to speak. The lines made no sense to him. The faces were gone.

Tears began to form in his eyes. He couldn't explain why he was so distressed. Rebecca, realizing that something had gone wrong, told him to close his eyes. He did as she asked. Very gently, she helped him once again to draw another face. He felt his hand moving guided by hers, felt the tip of the pen grazing the surface of the sheet of paper. He tried to follow the lines that she was making using his hand, but the only things that emerged in his imagination were abstract shapes. They continued tracing what she assured him was a face.

"This is the nose," she said.

"Yeah, I know that." His voice contained mild aggravation. She stared at him. "I'm sorry."

"Now we're going to do the eyes."

And they did the eyes. Then the ears, which were of a more complicated geometry than the rest of the face. They did the lips, the chin, the repetitive pattern of the hair. He knew exactly what was happening but failed to visualize anything.

When it was complete, he opened his eyes and looked at the sheet of paper. It surprised him. He saw a face on the sheet of paper. Thus encouraged, he took a fresh sheet of paper and attempted to do a drawing on his own. His confidence was quickly overtaken by panic. He had a face that he could see in his mind, but the only thing he could produce with the pen were up-and-down squiggles. He quickly realized what was happening. He was drawing fingers. In his alarm, he broke into tears.

Later, when they went to bed, he didn't sleep. He chose instead to simply hold her hand as he stared at the ceiling waiting for the break of dawn. He thought back to when they first met. It was at an academic conference in Taipei on a rainy morning three years before. As if to live up to some kind of cliché, they shared an umbrella that day. Monsoon season, someone told them. They just laughed. Their first conversations were about Wong Kar-wai. On their free days, they explored the city together. Then they said goodbye.

After the conference, they kept in touch and tried to overcome the distance between them. She liked to draw and sent him cards with watercolour paintings of flowers and animals, sometimes buildings. He had no such talents, but he sent along some bad origami from time to time. They tried meeting up again, once, then twice, in disparate places, and they said goodbye, once, then twice. Before they had realized it, they had begun to accrue their history of departures. There was a lunar quality to their relationship, the effects of distance and time intruding and then receding, like the billowing and waning of the clouds, like a curious tide. After two years, they decided that it was right, and it felt as though, like the planets, they had gone the long way round in order to return to one another. On that day, feeling indulgent, he quoted Cortázar and said to her: "We went around without looking for each other, but knowing we went around to find each other."

With their relationship, he had learnt that different types of love were possible, including one characterized by an impossible distance, where both parties were intimately close, and yet unquestionably apart.

Thinking back now, he was amazed that they managed to make it work somehow. Their relationship became characterized by short reunions and long stretches of yearning, punctuated by the empty promises of digital screens, held together with friendship, patience, and plain stubbornness. He believed at first that it would eventually wear them down, but together, they learnt that every goodbye was merely a promise of another hello, that every parting foreshadowed a return to each other's side. However, the definitions had changed. Certain that the next time that they parted would be the last, he wasn't sure if he was ready to say goodbye again. Thus confronted by the finality of farewell, he understood that the spectre of death had twisted the meanings of words. Words such as always, tomorrow, hello, and goodbye. On second thought, while it was a grim way of looking at it, it was death that had returned those words to their actual definitions, allowed them to achieve their true resonance.

Seven

The alarm rang at three in the morning. They got up and got ready for the long flight home. Rebecca made the coffee and Darryl made the cereal. After quickly showering, they did a check on all of their luggage, unplugged their charging phones, and called for a taxi. He didn't say goodbye to his Turkish programmer friend, but they left a card.

An unusual calm seemed to have seized the ride to the airport. The outside world looked strangely unfamiliar. The couple held hands, but didn't look at each other, as if they couldn't bear to. When they arrived, his eyes were drawn to the sheer brightness and mass of the buildings. The airport, it occurred to him then for some reason, probably looked much the same every hour of the day, every day of the year. Together, they proceeded past the automated glass doors. Something about the architecture disturbed him. There was something about its angular nature, its sharp lines, and the doubling of its geometry within the shadows. He thought that it may have been its predictability, its lack of surprise, the fact that the airport looked just as an airport would. It irked him that the floor was tiled in such a plain manner. There was no art in it, designed to invoke a nonspecific sense of pleasantness, forming a grid, a net, a tessellation.

They made their way to the counter to check in the

luggage. It was then that Rebecca reminded him to take the pills to pre-empt any case of airsickness. He nodded grimly and assured her that he would do so later. He didn't like taking pills, perhaps because to him they only seemed to underscore his mortality, but he had little choice if he wanted to be sure of avoiding an episode of nausea on the plane. He made a mental note to do so just as the airline staff handed them their boarding passes. He noticed just then that her face had vanished, and in its place was a clenched fist. She recited a generic message about having a good flight, and they said their thanks with tired smiles.

Collecting the rest of their luggage, Darryl turned to look out of the main doors. It was still dark outside. He took his time, certain that it was the last time he would see the city. He told himself that it was a way of bidding goodbye to a place that he had spent a significant fraction of what was probably the last year of his life in. They wandered around thereafter, shared a coffee, and then, having passed enough time, they made their way to the departure hall.

The officer studied Darryl's face for a long time, comparing it to the passport, which made him feel incredibly nervous. He had an anxiety issue with such things. Much in the same way he often imagined the alarm ringing upon leaving any store with an electronic security system. It wasn't that he fantasized about shoplifting, but that he had an unreasonable fear of being accused of crimes he did not commit. Finally, the officer let him pass. A security inspection followed, and he was greeted by a very stern-looking officer. The inspection was poorly managed; people were left not quite knowing where to go or what to do, their personal possessions scattered all over the place. This also irked him. *I'm almost dead*, he thought. *I don't have to put up with this.* So, pretending to be incredibly distressed, he collected his belt and shoes, his trousers nearly coming off, and dragged all of his belongings in an open suitcase in the most undignified manner possible.

Rebecca chided him for his childishness but laughed at how silly he looked. After he had collected himself, they went into the departure lounge. There was still more than an hour before the gate closed. To their left, they saw shops stretching to the end of the departure hall, surprisingly still open at this hour, each one an exercise in psychological design, from the arrangement of products to the precision of the lighting. To their right—trolleys, mass-manufactured geometrical shapes, metals removed from their site of mining, coffee joints, brands and logos, smells and similarities, and children. The children seemed faceless. He stopped. He blinked and spent a moment contemplating, making sure that it was only a thought. He looked again at the children. Their faces had yet to return.

Having nothing better to do, the couple decided to explore some of the shops. They spent a bit of time in a bookstore, browsing, chatting, saying meaningless things because they enjoyed doing so, or maybe because there wasn't anything else to do. They moved on to an electronics store. Then a fashion boutique. Darryl couldn't shake the feeling of monotony. He consoled himself with the thought that perhaps there was music to be found in the chatter and gossip, and in the children's voices, and in the background radio. Yet, there remained a type of rhythmic insistence so characteristic of humans. Studying the people in the shop—the businessman with suit and suitcase, the elderly woman with a cautious gait on her first holiday, the familiar expressions of teenage adventurers—he discovered all of the different faces belonged to the same person. Or perhaps the same faces belonged to different people. Even in their difference, these mannequins belonged to the hands of the same master. Monotony, he thought, a monotony that disgusted him.

This was not the disease. He knew it. It was not a biological or physiological phenomenon that he was experiencing. But perhaps his condition had contributed to this change in existential perspective. With cognition this unreliable, it made recognising the unfortunate tropes of living all the easier.

He thought about the journey as a whole, recalling a conversation several years ago where he described how he disliked being on a plane. He disliked the whole experience. He hated security checks because they often somehow felt demeaning to him. He didn't like being inspected like he was a criminal. It was dehumanizing. He also didn't like how each stamp and each visa was earned through the authority of external documents, reducing a person to a name, a face, a number, little more than his or her passport. It struck him as a situation in which identity was externalized. It wasn't that much of a stretch to imagine a person leaving this airport as one person and arriving at that airport as another—and nothingness in between. Every facet of travel seemed designed to prevent one from being substantial—of substance—and compounded the feeling of anonymity that he felt intensely while being on an airplane.

When he was younger, back when his creative aspirations were still alive, he wrote a lot of fiction. He once tried writing a short story about a man who struggled with this exact and admittedly irrational problem. It wasn't very good and it was no surprise that it didn't win the competition it was submitted to. But he remembered it fondly because it helped pin down a basic fear, that travelling explicated the otherwise slow-drip process of reconfiguration, where a person would leave one time, one identity to inhabit another. A new context, a new persona, a new face. The disconnect frightened him not because it was so pronounced, but because it was at the heart of the passage of time, underneath the seemingly coherent narrative of the everyday.

He never told Rebecca about the irrational and over-rationalized fear that he had of flight. He smiled at her unconvincingly, holding her hand more tightly as they moved towards the aircraft.

She didn't have to know, he reasoned. She was dealing with enough already. When they had found their seats, Darryl started to work on putting the hand-carry luggage in the overhead compartments. Sitting in front of them was a woman, a teenage girl. Across the aisle, there was an elderly and obese man with his wife, and in front of them, a child and her mother. When he sat down, he didn't look behind their seats.

The child intrigued him, wielding a pencil in the manner of a tyrant wielding words. At first, her sketches were nothing but disorganized lines, but with time, they became shapes, a circle, a triangle, a rectangle. Finally, she drew an impression of a man. However, dissatisfied with its invention, she removed it from the drawing. And as Darryl watched her apply eraser to paper, he saw his reflection in the pencil figure being gradually deleted. He averted his gaze.

The plane engaged in taxiing. Familiar announcements, safety procedures, prohibitions, seat belt buckles, physical forces that pushed him into his seat. He turned his phone off. And then he braced himself as the plane took off and rose into the blue nothing. Clouds unfurled in the manner of flowers. The sun was still rising. He learnt then that he couldn't tell the difference between the dawn and the gloaming.

The plane cruised along. It was proving to be a very quiet flight. There was no conversation between him and Rebecca. She was fast asleep next to him. He listened to the whir of the aircraft as he looked around the faceless cabin. The screen in front of him showed the flight details. Fleetingly, he considered putting a movie on, but didn't feel quite in the mood for it. Instead, he kept his diary out, keen to write more, yet not being able to find the words. He fiddled with the pen for a bit, but it offered no inspiration.

The plane continued its ascent. He looked around the cabin and was troubled to find that it had occurred again. He glanced towards the child and saw that her face had taken the form of an open palm.

He didn't check if it had happened to everyone. What did it matter? He didn't really want to know. He peered out of the window instead. Wisps of clouds drifted past. He looked down into the vast blue expanse and was briefly entranced by the tessellations of the waves, much like brushstrokes on an impossibly large canvas, or perhaps dancers in a carefully coordinated chaos. He studied the patterns intensely.

At first, the details were too small to make out, but the longer he stared at the waves, the clearer it seemed to become. He realized that he could deceive himself into believing that they traced out faces. This seemed preferable to the grotesque facelessness that had overtaken the aircraft cabin. He kept his gaze trained on these eddying faces, these painted swirls, these water-ghosts. He was entranced but also slightly afraid. As they continued shifting, they took on a terrible visage, a sea of wails unable to escape the maelstrom. Or perhaps they weren't struggling to break free as much as they were preparing to welcome him into the abyss. He wanted to call someone, ask someone to verify if it there was indeed an ocean stirring with such discord outside of his window. There was no way, he told himself, but he needed some kind of confirmation. He wanted to know if there was any truth to this distorted reality.

It was then that he put pen to paper. There was an urgency to his writing. He pushed the tip of the pen forcefully onto the page, as though he had to get the words down before they slipped away. It felt as though his hand was proceeding without instruction—at least, not from himself. He looked at the page but the sentences did not cohere.

What is the sea? It's people pushing past you, people disconnected. It's voices, fragmented and yet orchestrated, thoughts all different and yet so much the same. A monotonous patchwork of people who are not us. Strangers, friends, incomprehensible, inassimilable, legion. The sea leaves us adrift. We are the currents, the waves. We are the atoms that make its patterns. Our routines and practices guide its swirls and eddies. Faces in facelessness. The sea finds its monotony in our monotony, and we find our tedium in its tedium.

Nonsense. He had written nonsense. Senseless scribbling. Thus, having driven himself into a dead end, he stopped. It surprised him that he was breathing quickly. He looked out through the window at the vast blue nothing. Just then, it occurred to him that he hadn't taken his pills. He didn't even remember where he had left them. This made him slightly nervous, although he was careful about overreacting. It probably wasn't going to be a problem, but, then again, his recent episode of nausea didn't exactly inspire much confidence. He remembered being sick once on a cruise liner as a child when the family was on holiday. That wasn't a happy time. Of course, he was still feeling all right, and there was nothing to say that he couldn't make it through the long flight without incident. He checked the time. He'd made it through two and a half hours without issue. He wasn't entirely confident about keeping his winning streak going but felt that he would be able to get by if he tried.

He wanted to talk. He wanted to make a connection to someone, to anchor himself in someone else's mind. Maybe it would take his mind off of things. He looked to the girl lost in her pop music, now watching a movie, the attendant in his uniform, the generic name on the generic name tag, the child and her drawings, simply staring at them as if in search of some hidden meaning, Rebecca still asleep on his shoulder, and he realized that it was impossible.

Time made even less sense than usual. Everything seemed to have slowed to a crawl, but he looked at the clock on the screen in front of him, counted the seconds, and couldn't detect this deceleration. This mismatch disturbed him. He peered out of the window again. He thought he could see Singapore in the distance. It was impossible, of course, but he was keen to embrace this fantasy. The island seemed to be dissolving, its definition changing. There was no mistaking the distinctive diamond shape of his homeland. He knew all the grooves of the island's perimeter well. Yet, as he continued to gaze at this illusion, he saw its shape changing, now ambiguous, now ill-defined. The waters too began to shift. He thought he could see in them a field of hands. It was unpleasant but not unexpected. It filled him with a gentle despair. His blood felt thin. He clung on, but to what? And to what end? His vision was darkening, clouded. Adrift, going slowly, he mumbled under his breath before surrendering to the gloom. He could feel himself disappearing. His head lolling, he descended into an absence of worry, but also an absence of care. His mind relaxed its grip on his limbs, and then, fingers, hands, putting him to sleep. Anaesthesia. He couldn't recall if he had taken the pills. After all, how could he explain the drowsiness if he hadn't? Then thinking itself became a struggle. Tedium and torpor. And then, senselessness. He fell into a deep sleep, not even putting up a fight. He embraced the state of limbo, or perhaps it embraced him, crossing time zones, date lines, days and nights, the geography of time.

Acknowledgements

The first epigraph to this book is taken from the poem "Parca" by Salvador Espriu. This version is a translation from the Catalan by Louis J. Rodrigues found in Carcanet Press' 1997 collection *Salvador Espriu: Selected Poems*.

The second epigraph is from *The Hearing Trumpet* by Leonora Carrington © 1999 Leonora Carrington

I am grateful to Emily and Nilanjana for shepherding this book to publication.

I am indebted to Rachel for her work on the book's cover—as well as her friendship.

A number of these pieces went through various stages of development. Some pieces benefitted from the those who read works in progress, and others were revitalized after different collaborations. The manuscript itself saw numerous transformations over time. I am grateful for all the conversations, encouragement, ideas, and feedback that I've received in the life of this text—and all of that which is still to come.

Notes on Previous Publication

"A Secret Literature: The Literature of Ong Hwee Teng and the Possibilities of Disappearance" was the second prize winner of the Golden Point Award 2013.

A version of "Ghost" first appeared in *The Inventors* (Rosetta Cultures, 2023).